PLAYING WITH FIRE

HELLFIRE SERIES BOOK #5

ELLE JAMES

TWISTED PAGE INC

PLAYING WITH FIRE

HELLFIRE SERIES BOOK #5

With the added bonus of
HELLFIRE IN HIGHHEELS
The prequel to
PLAYING WITH FIRE

New York Times & USA Today
Bestselling Author

ELLE JAMES

ISBN EBOOK: 978-1-62695-220-1

ISBN PRINT: 978-1-62695-221-8

This book is dedicated to the firefighters of all kinds in all places. You are the heroes willing to risk your lives to save others.

Special thanks to Tim Gifford for sharing your stories and inspiring me to write this book. Thank you for your years as a firefighter. You are the stuff out of which heroes are made. Thank you to my wonderful editor Delilah Devlin and super quick proofreaders, Fedora, Reina, Rachel and Barb! You make my work shine!

Escape with...
Elle James
aka Myla Jackson

AUTHOR'S NOTE

Enjoy other books by Elle James

Hellfire Series
Hellfire, Texas (#1)
Justice Burning (#2)
Smoldering Desire (#3)
Hellfire in High Heels (#4)
Playing With Fire (#5)
Up in Flames (#6)
Total Meltdown (#7) TBD

Visit ellejames.com for more titles and release dates
For hot cowboys, visit her alter ego Myla Jackson at
mylajackson.com
and join Elle James and Myla Jackson's Newsletter at
Newsletter

HELLFIRE IN HIGHHEELS

HELLFIRE BOOK #4

Prequel to
Playing With Fire

New York Times & USA Today
Bestselling Author

ELLE JAMES

Hellfire In

Highheels

A HELLFIRE STORY

ELLE JAMES

CHAPTER 1

LOLA ENGEL FLIPPED the sign in the window of her shoe shop to display CLOSED and exited the building, pulling the door shut behind her. She locked it and glanced at her watch.

Damn.

She had only an hour to get home, change and stage an "accident" before Chance Grayson went off duty at the fire station.

Running in high heels was never good, nor classy. If at all possible, Lola avoided running in public. Scarred as a child by name-calling bullies, she didn't want anyone comparing her to an epileptic giraffe during a grand mal seizure. So, she hurried, skipping along, and then running all out when she verified no one was watching.

For a thirty-nine-year-old woman—okay, forty-three, though no one but her doctor knew the truth—she kept her body in top physical condition, with not an ounce of fat on her thighs or belly. Since her husband had passed, she'd had loads of time on her hands. Time she preferred to fill working out or flirting with the best-looking man in Hellfire, Texas.

Chance Grayson. One of the four Grayson brothers, all of whom were incredibly clean-cut, drool-worthy, butt-hugging, jean-clad cowboys and firefighters. They'd struck it rich in the gene pool, and Lola wouldn't mind having some of that gold stretched out in her bed.

Oh, she wasn't looking for long-term commitment or love. She'd already been in love once and losing someone you cared for as much as she'd cared for Mr. Engel hurt far too much.

No, she'd vowed to enjoy an active sex life with whomever the hell she pleased, and screw the tongue-wagging, back-stabbing biddies of the community who thought they were better than anyone else because they were married and settled.

Settled only meant living in a rut. Lola refused to slip on a ring or into a rut. Losing her husband had taught her one valuable lesson: *Life was too damned short.* She had to seize it by the balls and hold on to that orgasmic finish line.

Two blocks down, two to go. Why the hell had she walked to work that morning? And why the hell hadn't she worn tennis shoes?

Because you're too goddamn vain and won't let others see you in anything less than the most expensive shoes this side of the Mississippi.

New York City didn't have anything on Hellfire, Texas. Lola made damn sure of that. If she didn't sell many expensive shoes in her brick-and-mortar store, she sold a truckload every week from her online shop.

4

Just because a person lived in small-town, snail's-paced Texas didn't mean a woman had to deprive herself of the best and sexiest shoes from some of the most fabulous designers this world had to offer.

Slowly, but surely, she'd educated the ranchers' wives on the difference between Jimmy Choos stilettoes and Ariat cowboy boots. Not many of the wives had the kind of money for the more expensive brands, but Lola stocked budget knock-offs to satisfy the locals.

At that moment, she would trade her Jimmy Choos for some running shoes. All because she wanted a shot at seducing Chance Grayson. The younger man had caught her eye the day she'd seen him shirtless hosing down his big, red fire truck.

The day had been a typical hotter-than-Hades summer one in Texas. Sweat had glistened on the young man's shoulders, and all Lola could think was how she wanted to run her hands over every part of Chance's body. Then she'd start all over with her tongue.

Who said a woman of thirty-nine had to settle for men her own age? Forty-year-old men dated twenty-somethings all the time. Lola was a heck of a lot better in bed than most of those little girls. She could show Chance Grayson a thing or two. She just had to get his attention.

So far, she was zero for three in her attempts. She'd picked days she knew he was on duty to call 911 for help only the fire station, and his particular truck, would respond to.

Finding a kitten to strand high in a tree had been a challenge. Chance had been the first responder. Lola had dressed in a low-cut, midriff blouse, showing off her buoyant breasts and flat belly. She'd worn the strappy, pink Christian Louboutins.

Chance had saved the kitten and left, without giving her a second look.

The worst part of that incident had been his partner, Flannigan, who'd frowned, his gaze raking her from top to bottom. But not in a good way. "You'll break an ankle in those," he'd said and left, shaking his head.

The red-haired, tattooed, motorcycle-riding bear of a man hadn't known squat about the high-end shoes she wore.

Lola had been mad enough to throw one of her pricey shoes at the back of the man's head. Then when she'd leaned against the tree, holding the squirming kitten, a bee stung her in the ass.

Still, that hadn't been the end of her woes.

She'd jumped way from the tree, came short of launching the kitten into outer space, and stepped in a pile of dog poop. *In her Christian Louboutins!*

All that trouble, and Chance hadn't given her even a wink. Now, she had a ruined pair of very expensive stilettoes and a cat named Flannigan. Yes, she'd named the cat after the asshat Flannigan with the intention of kicking it every time she remembered that day, her failure, and the ruined shoes.

Fortunately for Flannigan the kitten, Lola didn't have the heart to hurt it. Hell, she'd never much cared for cats and had refused to get one, afraid she'd be labeled a lonely cat lady. And, to top things off, the darned kitten had taken up residence on her pillow at night, half-lying on her head.

Lola would never tell a soul that she kind of liked the little guy. She sure as hell wouldn't tell Flannigan, the tattooed firefighter. He'd laugh her all the way to the Jimmy Choo shoe factory in the UK.

His obvious derision of her shoes and her attempt to capture Chance's attention made her even more determined to snag the Grayson brother. She was older, but far from dead, and in the hormone-humming, sexual prime of her life.

The second attempt had been an equal failure when she'd deliberately jammed the electronic locks in her old car and called 911, asking for them to bring the Jaws of Life.

Sheriff's Deputy Leamon and the fire truck arrived. Chance had been there, but he'd stood back while the deputy slipped a flat tool down her window into the door and unlocked it in like two seconds flat.

By the time she'd stepped out of her vehicle in Manolo Blahnik spikes—which should have snapped the man's head around—her efforts had been wasted on Lenny the sweet, but clueless sheriff's deputy, who couldn't have been more than eighteen years old. Okay, maybe twenty.

Burning leaves had been another disaster. Yes, she'd done right by calling the sheriff's office to tell them she'd be burning. A little while later, she'd called 911 to say her fire was getting out of control, and she'd nearly burned down her garage in the process.

Chance had been one of two firemen who'd gotten there first. Flannigan had been the other, much to Lola's disgust.

While Chance had unrolled the giant firehose, Flan-

7

nigan put out the fire with Lola's garden hose. When Chance saw Flannigan had it under control, he'd folded and fitted the giant hose back onto the truck.

Meanwhile, the odious Flannigan, carrying her garden hose, had stopped in front of her. "Why didn't you keep your garden hose handy?"

Disgruntled at the man for ruining her third attempt, she'd glared and said the first thing to come to her mind. "I certainly didn't want to get my shoes wet."

That day she'd been careful to rake the leaves while wearing worn work boots. But when it came time to burn the leaves, she'd changed into a sexy leopard-print, off-the-shoulder shorts romper and her matching Salvatore Ferragamo, lace-up, espadrille wedges.

She'd stomped her wedge-heeled foot. "And why are you always with Chance? Why can't he come alone?"

"Is that what this is all about?" Flannigan-the-Bastard had shaken his head. "Woman, you have to stop calling 911. The sheriff can arrest you for wasting our time." He'd shot a derisive sneer at her feet. "And get some real shoes for when you're burning leaves in your yard." As he'd handed her the garden hose, he'd squeezed the handle, sending a spray of water onto her beautiful shoes.

Lola had squealed, dropped the hose, and hopped away. Unfortunately, the handle had jammed in the open position, and the hose twisted and spun like a snake on speed. Before she'd caught the hose, her sexy romper was soaked, the hairstyle she'd spent hours perfecting was equally drenched and lying limp around her face. Her makeup had run in rivulets down her cheeks, but that still hadn't been the worst of it. Her lace-up espadrille wedges were now covered in mud and falling apart.

All because of one tattooed jerk of a firefighter.

Not to mention, Lola had run out of reasons to call the fire department, short of setting her house on fire.

Until today. At lunch, she'd stopped by the station to drop off a batch of cookies for the guys and had learned that her nemesis, Flannigan, had taken the day off to work on some construction project. Chance had been outside, washing the ladder truck. That's when it hit her. The idea that would give Chance the opportunity to save her, and she'd show him her appreciation in such a way he couldn't resist.

She just had to get home in time to catch Chance before he went off shift.

Lola reached home with twenty minutes to spare. She rushed inside, almost tripped over the kitten, and set her purse on the counter. Quickly changing into a pair of shorts, too short to be legal, and a miniscule button-down top that bared most of her midriff—because the air was hot, and it was Texas. *Uh-huh*. Not to mention, this partic-ular, scoop-necked top was so tight it gave her breasts extra lift and displayed them to their best advantage.

Back out to the garage, she ran, found the ladder that had hung in the same spot since her husband had died more than six years ago, and hurked it off the hooks. Heavier than she'd expected, it nearly clobbered her. But Lola was determined. This might be her best opportunity to capture the Grayson hunk's attention. And she'd gone a long time without sex. She'd worn out two battery-operated-boyfriends. The time had come to have someone in her bed.

Back to the house, she set up the extension ladder and climbed up to the roof. She was all right, until she looked down. Two stories didn't look like much when your feet were steady on the ground. But looking down...

She swayed, her pulse pounded and her breaths came in shallow gasps. If she weren't careful, she'd hyperventilate and fall off the roof before Chance could save her.

Hauling in a deep breath, she sat back on the shingles, pressed her ankle-strap Prada sandal against the ladder and gave it a shove.

It leaned out and came back.

Damn it.

She did it again, giving it a heftier push.

This time the ladder swung away from the roof then teetered precariously between falling toward the roof or away. For a moment, Lola thought it would come back toward her. She held her breath and nearly cheered when the ladder fell to the ground.

Congratulating herself on achieving the first part of the plan, she pulled her cellphone from her back pocket.

After poking her manicured nails at 9-1-1, she waited. Even before the first ring, she could hear the blare of sirens. She frowned. How could they already know she needed help?

Then a terrible thought occurred. The fire department was being deployed to an actual emergency...

CHAPTER 2

DANIEL FLANNIGAN STOPPED by the fire station on his way home from the house where he'd been working for an older woman whose husband had passed away. Her roof had begun to leak, and she couldn't afford to pay a contractor to fix it.

Daniel had heard about her through one of the members of his motorcycle club who lived on the same block. They'd planned a day when they could all be off to do the repairs the woman needed.

With ten people from his club there, they'd put in a full day's effort and completed all the work they'd set out to do, plus a few other fix-it items they'd discovered along the way.

Feeling good about what they'd accomplished, Daniel stopped by the fire station to see if any of the guys wanted to grab a beer at the Ugly Stick Saloon when they got off shift.

The men for the next shift were already arriving when

Daniel pulled into the parking lot, a ladder and his power tools still in the back of this pickup.

Chance Grayson ran out of the building toward the pumper truck, shrugging into his fire-retardant jacket as he raced across the concrete.

"What's going on?" Daniel called out.

"Old man Ford caught his pavilion on fire with his barbeque grill."

"Got enough men to handle it?"

"Yeah, between the two shifts, we've got it covered."

The fire chief stepped out of building, shaking his head. "Got a minor emergency—a woman trapped on her roof with no way to get down." He shook his head. "Hate to tie up anyone when that fire might get out of control." He cast a glance at Daniel. "What are you doing here? I thought you took the day off."

"I did," Daniel said and jerked a thumb over his shoulder. "I've got a ladder. Do you want me to check out the lady on the roof?"

"Would you?" The fire chief handed him a piece of paper. "I want to stick around in case they call for more help with the pavilion fire. I might get out the tanker truck and follow them to Ford's place."

Daniel shook his head. "Go. I can help the woman down."

"Thanks." The chief hurried toward the tanker truck parked at the rear of the station.

So much for a beer with his buddies. Daniel glanced down at the writing on the paper and groaned.

Not again.

He recognized the address, having been there with

Chance on three previous occasions over the past six months.

Lola Engel lived there, and she came up with the lamest excuses to call out the fire department.

After the first couple times, Daniel had seen through her *emergencies*. The woman had the hots for his buddy, Chance Grayson. Chance hadn't clued in, probably because Lola wasn't his usual kind of woman. Oh, he treated her with the kindness and respect due an older woman.

Unfortunately for Lola.

But seriously, crying wolf for the fourth time? This bullshit had to end. Since Chance couldn't see what was happening, Daniel would have to take matters into his own hands and tell the woman to stop.

While the fire trucks headed out of town, Daniel drove his pickup to Lola's house a little over two blocks away, thinking of the words he'd use to put the woman in her place. As he pulled into her yard, he almost laughed out loud.

What woman in her right mind climbed onto a roof wearing stilettoes? Only one woman he knew—Lola Engel.

He got out of his truck and started to unload his ladder when he spied an extension ladder lying in the grass.

"Oh, mother, please tell me it's not true," she muttered from above.

"What's not true?"

"I call for a real hero, and I get you."

His lips quirked at the corners. He always got a great

deal of pleasure out of calling her bluffs. This time would be no different. He glanced up at two slender, well-toned and tanned thighs, hanging over the edge of the roof. "Ms. Engel, are you all right up there?"

"Yes, of course I am," she snapped as she peered downward. "I just can't get down. Could you please put up the ladder? That's all I need. Then I can climb down by myself."

His grin stretched at her disgruntled tone. "Toss down those shoes, and I'll think about it."

"Are you out of your mind?" she asked, her eyes wide. "You don't *toss* a pair of Prada onto the ground from two stories up."

He fisted his hands on his hips. "You do if you want to get down off the roof. I'm not giving you the ladder until you lose those ridiculous shoes."

She frowned. "Do you promise to catch them?"

"Hell, no."

"Then I'm not dropping them." She crossed her arms over her chest. Without her hands on the roof, she slipped a few inches. Her eyes widened, and she slapped both palms flat on the shingles. "Okay, okay." With one hand on the roof, she slipped the straps off the backs of her heels. Then she leaned toward the edge and held out her hand with the shoes dangling from her fingertips. "Are the bushes right below my hand?"

"Seriously?" Daniel shook his head. "Yes, the bushes are below your hand. Now, drop the shoes before you fall and break your damn neck."

Lola pouted. "You don't have to be so grumpy. Do you have any idea how much these cost?"

"No," he bit out, his jaw tightening. "But they sure as hell aren't worth your life."

"That's your opinion." She sighed. "Here goes. But if they're damaged, I'm blaming you."

"Blame me. I don't give a rat's ass."

Lola let go of the shoes then released a breath.

No doubt she'd listened for a thunk and had been reassured when her shoes' fall was cushioned by the azalea bushes. Again, he shook his head.

Good for his word, Daniel propped the extension ladder against the eaves and started up.

"What are you doing?" she asked.

Daniel hid a smile. "Saving a damsel in distress."

"I told you, I can climb down on my own."

"You'd deprive a knight in shining armor from doing his duty?" He didn't slow until he reached the top.

Lola snorted and muttered beneath her breath, "Knight, my pearly-white ass."

Daniel stopped near the top and took a moment to admire the picture she made in her tiny shorts and top. The woman was flashing more skin than most women did on a beach. "Do you want off this roof or not?"

Lola bit her bottom lip. "Well, since you're here…I guess you can help." She eased to the edge. "Climbing up was a lot easier than getting back down." She chewed on her lip as she scooted her bottom along the shingles to the edge.

"Turn over and lie on your stomach. I'll guide your feet to the first rung."

She frowned. "Are you sure that'll work?"

"Positive." He snapped his fingers, impatiently. "Hurry up. I don't have all day."

"Bossy much?" she groused and did as he said.

With her bottom in the air and her legs within reach, she presented Daniel a different perspective than he was used to. Instantly, he developed a great appreciation for her *pearly-white ass*. "You shouldn't climb up ladders without someone to spot you, Ms. Engel." He wrapped a hand around one trim ankle and guided her pretty foot to the rung. "You could fall and break those sexy legs."

"What did you say?" She jerked around and almost slid off the roof, taking him with her.

"Hey, watch what you're doing!" Daniel steadied her with his hands on her silky thighs then eased the other foot onto the ladder in front of him.

"You shouldn't say things like that when you have a woman in such a precarious situation."

"Well, it's true." He wrapped an arm around her and held onto the ladder.

"Which part? The part about falling, or the part about my sexy legs?" she asked, her attention on the rungs in front of her face.

"Both," he said against her hair. "Now, I'll take a step, and then you can take a step."

One rung at a time, they eased down the ladder. The entire way, Daniel inhaled the scent of honeysuckle. He glanced at the ground, searching for the source, but couldn't find one. That's when he realized what smelled was Lola.

He inhaled, startled at the lust coiling in his groin.

Shit, the woman had to be ten or twelve years older than him.

And probably had a lot of experience in bed.

Daniel shook his head. Forget it. She had a thing for his partner, Chance.

Her tight ass bumped into his belly several times on the way down, causing more discomfort in his tightening jeans.

What the hell? The woman was a nuisance. She liked crying wolf just to catch the attention of a man so much younger. And Chance didn't have a clue, nor would he appreciate a woman like Lola. "Do you work out or something?" Daniel asked, before he could stop himself.

"Every day. Since my husband died, I've taken up yoga and running. Why do you ask?"

"It shows."

"Oh." She paused for a second, and then continued, "Well, thank you."

When they reached the ground, Daniel stepped back, his body hot, his pulse pounding. "Ms. Engel, you've got to stop calling 911. One of these days, you'll have a real emergency, and no one will take you seriously."

She stared up at him, her eyes wide with fake innocence. "I really couldn't get off the roof."

Daniel narrowed his eyes. "I know what you're up to."

"I don't know what you're talking about." She spun away to retrieve her shoes from the bushes.

"Chance Grayson is not that into you," Flannigan pointed out.

Eyes narrowed, Lola lifted her chin. "He will be."

Daniel shook his head. "Why would he be? I mean, you're probably old enough to be his mother."

Lolo spun on Daniel. "You need to take that back, right now. I'd have to have given birth when I was a small child myself. And what's wrong with a younger man dating an older woman?"

"Well..." Daniel rubbed the back of his neck while he looked around for an escape. "It's just that older women aren't as attractive to younger men."

"Is that so?" She stepped up to him, pressing her breasts against his chest. "Are you saying you don't find me attractive?"

"Now, don't go puttin' words in my mouth. I told you that you have sexy legs. I don't say that about just anyone. Besides, you shouldn't go fishin' for compliments. You might not be happy with what you catch."

"No?" With a catlike smile stretching her lips, Lola walked a finger up his chest and over his chin. "What if I like what I catch?"

He grabbed her finger in his big hand. "You like Grayson. Leave me out of this."

"A woman has a right to change her mind." She pulled the hand he held toward her and pressed it to her chest, running his knuckles across the swells of her breasts. "And just so you know, they're real." She winked up at him and pressed her hips against his.

Damned if his cock didn't rise to the occasion.

Flannigan stared into her gaze, fighting to keep his hands from clasping her thighs and wrapping her sexy legs around his waist. Finally, he settled on grabbing her arms and pushing her to arm's length, away from his growing erection. "Woman, you're really playing with fire, here."

"Oh, I'm not afraid of getting burned." Lola batted her eyes, swept her tongue across her full, luscious lips and tilted her chin in challenge. "Are you?"

Something inside Flannigan snapped. "Fuck no," he muttered. With his hands still on her arms, he slammed her to his chest and crushed his mouth over hers.

At first blaming it on her taunting, his kiss was angry, vengeful and harsh. But the sweet, minty taste of her mouth and that damned scent of honey-suckle wrapped around his senses. He skimmed the seam of her lips with his tongue.

When she gasped and dropped her shoes, he thrust through, caressing her mouth with fevered strokes, imitating the age-old motion of mating. His dick responded, growing so hard Flannigan could barely breathe.

At first rigid, Lola's body was like a brick against his, her hands pressed flat against his chest. As the kiss continued, she softened, and then leaned into him. She raised her hands, entwining them around his neck to pull him closer.

What had started as a lesson in his ability to control the situation, ended in Flannigan getting schooled by the teacher.

CHAPTER 3

HOLY HOT TAMALES! Lola's body turned traitor. She'd tempted the big firefighter out of a need to prove he was wrong and prove that an older woman could be every bit as sexy as a younger one. What she hadn't expected was for him to go along with it. And she certainly hadn't expected to like it.

Once the kiss began, she had every intention of being the one to break it off and laugh in his face. But, *holy guacamole!* Now, she wasn't sure she needed to breathe as much as she needed Flannigan's lips on hers. In fact, she couldn't seem to get close enough to the man. Too many inches were between them, though their bodies were pressed together. No, inches weren't the problem.

Clothes were.

She slid her calf around the back of his and upward, until her crotch straddled his thick thigh. Her pussy ached for more, and rubbing against him only increased the heat.

After what felt like a lifetime and yet must have been

only a moment, Flannigan lifted his head and stared down into her gaze. His big, rough hands had migrated along her back. His eyes narrowed at the same time his fingers tightened around her ass.

Lola's head spun, and her lips throbbed. Her breathing was labored as if she'd been running a marathon. Through the fog of her thoughts, one emerged, *Burn, baby burn.*

She swallowed hard and went for bravado. "What's the matter, big guy? Never kiss a *real* woman, before?"

"I've kissed plenty of women," he said. "Some more experienced than you."

"Yeah, did they make you lose control?" she asked, liking the feel of his hands on her buttocks—warm, hard, and strong.

"I'm always in control," he said, his brows dipping.

"Uh-huh." She nodded toward the house across the street. "Do you always prefer an audience when you kiss a woman?"

Flannigan shot a glance over his shoulder at Lola's neighbor.

Mr. Harden was the nosey old man she loved to flash when he spied on her through his binoculars.

Flannigan glared at the man. "What the hell?"

"Mr. Harden's harmless. He just likes to watch." She tilted her head, a smile twitching at the edges of her lips. "Care to come in for a glass of iced tea? It's the least I can offer after you rescued me from the rooftop."

He hesitated, and then shook his head. "I should get going." He released her bottom and stepped back.

Lola resisted the urge to sink her fingernails into his arms. Instead, she stepped back as well and shrugged.

"Suit yourself." She turned and glanced over her shoulder. "Is Chance on duty tomorrow?" She knew perfectly well he was, along with Flannigan.

The firefighter frowned. "I meant what I said. You have to stop calling 911 unless it's a real emergency."

Lola stooped to grab the shoes she'd dropped, giving Flannigan and Mr. Harden an extra-sexy glimpse of her bottom beneath the hem of the shorts.

Something very much like a growl sounded behind her.

"Damn it, woman." Flannigan said. "Grayson isn't into you."

She turned and raised an eyebrow. "And you are?"

"I didn't say that," he muttered.

"Good, because I don't think you're man enough for a woman like me."

His chest swelled, and his eyes flared. "And what the hell is that supposed to mean?"

Lola raked her gaze over him from the top of his head to his boots, taking in the tattoos, the dirty jeans, and ripped T-shirt stretching impossibly tight over his broad chest.

Her heart thumped hard against her chest, but she forced calm to her face. "Seems like a man with tattoos is covering up something or compensating for what he lacks in other areas." She shot a meaningful glance at his package.

She had no doubt the man was equipped, based on the impressive bulge beneath the denim. And no doubt he was proud of it, like most men.

When she raised her face to his, she swallowed a gasp.

Anger blazed from his eyes. "My tattoos have nothing to do with compensation."

She shrugged. "So you say." Lola turned and walked away, placing one foot in front of the other for maximum hip action. "Don't let me keep you. I'm sure you have younger women to impress with your…manliness. I'll take my *chances* on a real man."

A more sinister growl sounded behind her, and the next thing Lola knew, a heavy hand yanked her around, and she was flung over a broad shoulder. Strong arms clamped like vices around her thighs.

"Hey! Put me down!" Lola braced her hands on his back and pushed against rock-hard muscles.

Flannigan didn't slow as he marched toward her front door.

With her gut being jounced on his shoulder, Lola could barely catch her breath. "Let…me…down…you Neanderthal." She pounded his back.

The beast came to an abrupt halt.

Lola pushed herself farther upright and caught a glimpse of Mr. Harden staring at the couple, wide-eyed.

"Let me down, or I'll scream," Lola said. "Mr. Harden is watching us. He'll call the sheriff and have your ass arrested for molesting me."

"You wish." He shoved open her door, turned and waved at Mr. Harden. "She didn't want to walk barefoot," he called out loud enough for the older man to hear. Then he slapped a heavy palm against Lola's bottom, hard enough to make her jump.

She should have been angry, but the smack had an entirely different effect.

Desire coiled in the pit of her belly, and her thighs burned where his hand and arm held her tightly.

Having a strong, sexy firefighter throw her over his shoulder and carry her away to make mad, passionate love was every woman's dream.

But Flannigan was the wrong firefighter.

He stepped inside and shoved the door closed behind him with his boot. "Apologize," he demanded.

"For what?" Lola wiggled. "You've made your point. You're a caveman. You have muscles." *And a great ass.*

"Is Chance's ass why you're so hot on him?"

Lola bit her lip. "Did I say ass out loud?"

"Yeah, and you still haven't apologized."

"For what? Calling it as I see it?"

His grip tightened. "For bad-mouthing my tattoos."

"Put me down, and I might just give you that apology." Now that Lola had noticed his firm butt in the faded jeans, she couldn't stop staring. Just when she considered lowering her hands down his back to touch him there, he hiked her up in the air and dropped her body to cradle her in his arms.

The movement placed her face so close to his, she only had to turn her head a little and her lips would be within kissing distance.

"The apology?" he prompted.

Lola raised her gaze from his lips and stared into his eyes, her pulse hammering, pushing hot blood through her veins. "What?"

"Apology? Tattoos?"

Flannigan didn't even break a sweat holding her above the ground. Lola shifted her gaze from his eyes to the view of his chest at the V of his neckline. "Why so touchy about the tats?"

"They hold special meaning."

She huffed. "Of your old girlfriends?"

"No, of the men I fought with in the Army. The men who came back in body bags."

Lola looked up, guilt twitching in her gut. "I'm sorry. I didn't know."

He nodded and dropped her feet to the ground, retaining his grip around her waist. "Now, you do."

Lola traced the little bit of a tattoo she could see on his chest and neck. "Those men must have meant a lot."

"They were my brothers." He caught her finger and lifted it to his lips. "Promise me you won't call 911 unless you have an emergency." Holding her gaze, he pressed his mouth to the tip of her finger.

Her finger tingled where his lips touched it. A spark flowed from that point all the way south, making her pussy clench. "What are you doing?"

"Oh, this?" He kissed her finger again. "It's best that I focus on your hand."

"As opposed to focusing on what?"

"What I really want to do."

Her heart fluttered then pounded against her ribs. She curled her fingers and dragged her nails down the front of his chest. "Aren't you afraid I'll ravage your body?"

He shook his head. "No, I'm afraid I'll do this." Flannigan scooped her up by the backs of her thighs, wrapped her legs around his waist and turned to press her against the wall. His mouth crashed down on hers, stealing away her breath.

Who needs to breathe, anyway? Lola wrapped her arms around his neck and clung to him, her tongue meeting his in a duel for supremacy. She locked her legs around his waist and sank lower, rubbing her pussy across the bulge of his cock. She wanted much more than a kiss.

While he kissed her, she grabbed a handful of his T-shirt and dragged it up his body.

Flannigan lifted his head, fisted his shirt in his hand and ripped it over his head, flinging it to the floor.

He worked at the tiny buttons of her shirt.

Frustrated, Lola pushed aside his hands and freed the last button.

The firefighter pushed her shirt off her shoulders then nipped and kissed her collarbone, her chin, and the sensitive area below her ear.

Lola leaned her head to the side, giving him better access, while shrugging out of the shirt. Once free, she inhaled, her chest rising.

Flannigan accepted the invitation and rolled her nipple between his teeth, through the lacy cup of her bra.

A moan rose up in Lola's throat, and she tightened her legs around him.

He pushed one of her bra straps over her shoulder and followed it downward, leaving a trail of kisses and nips.

"What are you doing to me?" she asked, every inch of her body on fire.

A low, warm chuckle rumbled in his chest. "If you don't know by now, you're not the experienced woman you claim to be."

"I'll show you experience," she said, making room between her hips and his. She reached for the button of his jeans and thumbed it open. Then she lowered the zipper halfway and slipped her hand beneath the denim. Her lips twitching, she looked up into his face. "Commando?"

He drew in a sharp breath, leaned closer and whispered against her neck. "The only way to go." The firefighter tongued the pulse beating at the base of her throat.

"Mmm, yes," she said as she curled her hand around his cock and pushed lower to cup his balls.

He placed his hand over hers. "Don't tease."

She rolled his sac in her fingers, her gaze seeking his dark eyes. "Does this feel like I'm teasing?"

"Some women like to take a man to the edge and leave him hanging."

"Sweetheart, I'm not one of them." She squeezed gently, and then slid her hand up his cock. "I don't start anything I'm not willing to finish."

"Good." He gripped her ass and carried her to the kitchen, swept the salt and pepper shakers off the table with his arm, and set her bottom on the edge. Then he stood back, the motion forcing her to remove her hand from his jeans.

Lola frowned. "Are you teasing me now?"

"No, but I want you to know an experienced woman has nothing on me." His brows descended. "Say no now, and I'll walk away."

"Or?" She parted her legs and rubbed her fingers over her pulsing pussy. God, she was hot. The intensity of Flannigan's expression made her want to strip off the rest of her clothes and jump on his dick.

Sweet Jesus, she'd gone far too long without sex. She lifted her chin and waited for his next move.

"*Or*, I'm going to blow your mind."

"Blow, baby, blow." Lola arched her back and released the catch on her bra. For a moment, she wondered if the slight sag to her breasts would turn off a younger man who'd probably seen more women with perky, young breasts than Lola had seen naked men.

If she hadn't been studying his face, she might have missed the slight flare of his eyes as the bra fell away.

By the expression on his face, the man wasn't turned off. In fact, his zipper had slipped lower, and his cock sprang free, jutting straight out—hard, thick and ready.

Flannigan bent over her and pressed his lips to her nipple. He sucked it into his mouth and rolled the tip on his tongue. Then he nipped.

"Ouch!" She laced her fingers into his hair and pulled. "Those are attached."

He moved to the other and licked the nipple into a tight bead. "I noticed." Then he drew it into his mouth and sucked hard.

Lola moaned and clutched the back of his head, urging him to take as much of her breast into his mouth as he could.

He laved, sucked and nibbled until she squirmed on the tabletop.

Without raising his head, he urged her to lie back on the table. As he blazed a trail over her ribs and down her abdomen with his mouth, his hands worked the button loose on her shorts and slipped the garment down her legs. The shorts fell to the floor, leaving only a lace thong covering her sex.

The firefighter slipped his fingers beneath the elastic band, and he cupped her sex, dipping a finger into her pussy.

Lola moaned and spread her legs.

His hand was hot against her skin. His finger felt so good. But, it wasn't enough. Lola squirmed again, laid a hand over his and pressed him closer, encouraging him to fit more of his fingers inside her.

He obliged, swirling around the juices.

Lola moaned.

"Like that?" he asked.

"I might," she said, her tone tight, her breathing ragged.

Then he edged her panties lower, parted her folds, and blew a warm stream of air over her clit.

Lola gasped and came up on her elbows. "For Pete's sake, don't tease me!"

"Do you want more?" he asked, his thumbs looping through the straps of her thong.

"Yes!" she managed to say on a rush of air.

He ripped off the panties, wedged himself between her thighs and dropped to his knees.

Oh, sweet heaven, the man *did* know what a woman wanted.

Lola lay back on the table, grasping the edge, prepared to experience the joys of sex.

Flannigan parted her folds and stroked one long, work-roughened finger across her clit and down to her damp entrance.

Tossing her head, Lola gasped, "Oh, my."

He chuckled. "Hit the spot?"

"Oh, *yesss!*"

The rumble of his laughter was offset a second later by a cool stream of air blown over her heated center.

Lola's breath hitched and held in anticipation of what might come next. She wasn't disappointed when he flicked her clit with his tongue.

Lola arched her back off the table and clung to his hair. "Sweet tea and grits, that's the spot. Oh, yes! That's the spot."

"Thought it might be," he said, his breath warm against her pussy.

With that wonderful tongue, he teased, tapped and twirled the sensitive nubbin, until tingling started at her center and shot out to the farthest reaches of her extremities, sizzling a path of nerves to the point Lola tipped over the edge, her body tense and throbbing with her orgasm.

He didn't let up his ministrations until she lay back against the table, as limp as a dishrag, too spent to move a muscle but not ready for the encounter to be over.

A chuckle rose with Flannigan as he straightened between her legs, his cock jutting forward, hard and thick.

Though movement was a struggle, Lola managed to push herself up onto her elbows. She refused to be outdone by the sassy firefighter. He might have proved he was capable of making her squeal, but she was up to the challenge. "I call your bet and raise the ante." She slipped off the edge of the table, thinking she'd never be able to look at it as purely a place for eating food again. Eating, yes. Food, not so much.

With as much grace as she could muster, she stood, naked and proud, and held out her hand. "Protection?"

Flannigan's brows furrowed then lifted. "Oh, yeah." He pulled his wallet from his pocket and extracted a condom, handing it to her. Then he tossed the wallet on the table.

She held the foil packet in her hand for a moment, and then turned on her bare heel and walked toward her bedroom, giving him her backside, naked from head to toe. She knew her body wasn't a young twenty-something, but she was fit, her muscles were well-defined and tight. She could bounce a quarter off her abs. She knew, because she'd tried it.

She'd taken a total of five steps when a growl sounded behind her, and she was scooped off her feet and carried at a much-quicker pace to the bedroom at the back of the apartment.

She lay an arm over his shoulders and quirked an eyebrow. "You know I can walk like normal people."

"You're not normal, and you walk too slowly," he said, his tone raspy.

His grip on her felt tight to the point of almost painful. A thrill of excitement ripped through Lola. This was a man who knew passion and kept it under control. Her challenge was to shake his control.

Once he passed through her bedroom door, Flannigan tossed her on the bed and stood back. "I have to go."

What the hell? Lola blinked, her only outward reaction to his announcement. From the look of his narrowed eyes, this had been his plan all along. Thinking quickly, she knew she had to use the big guns to make this man stay and service her.

She rolled onto her side and slid the condom package from her hip up to the curve of her breast, and then flicked the tip of a nipple with the package. "Sure you won't stay a little longer and put this little gem to use?"

"I have better things to do," he said, though his gaze followed the path of the foil square.

Moving her hand, she brushed the condom across her belly and down to the juncture of her thighs, and then slowly rolled to her back. "Better?" She raised her brows, not that he was looking at her face.

His cock was as hard and straight as a tire iron, ready to jack her up.

Lola eased off the bed. "Let me show you to the door, since you're in a hurry to leave." She stopped in front of him and danced her fingers across his bare chest and downward, skimming over his ribs, past his belly button, following the arrow of hair to the thatch disappearing into his sagging jeans. His cock jerked in anticipation of her touch.

Yeah, he wanted her, but why was he fighting that most natural of urges?

Lola refused to let him leave before she'd had her way with him. Starting with his dick. She wrapped her fingers around it and tugged gently. "Unless you can think of another reason to stay a little longer."

His jaw flexed with tension. "I really need to leave."

She nodded and gave him a fake pout. "I understand. Say hello to Chance." She reached lower and cupped his balls. "No, I'll tell him myself."

Flannigan stood still, his breaths coming in rapid,

shallow intakes. He gripped her arms and lowered her to her knees.

Lola didn't fight the commanding movement. This was where she'd planned to be even if he hadn't placed her there.

The thrill of anticipation made her pulse beat faster. She knelt before him, her face in front of his cock. "No going back now." She touched the tip of his shaft with her tongue.

A droplet of come slipped out.

Lola licked it off, loving the musky flavor of him. Then she traced the head of his penis at an excruciatingly slow pace, paying him back for giving her a condom, and then threatening to leave without using it.

No effing way.

Her core ached with a need only his hard shaft could satisfy. He wasn't going anywhere until he'd taken her to a higher point in the stratosphere.

No, sir.

And she wouldn't let him go until she'd rocked his world so completely, he'd wish he was Chance Grayson, the man of her lust-filled dreams.

Lola wrapped her lips around the tip of his cock and touched her tongue to the tip, swirling around its velvety smoothness. Then she let go.

His chest swelled on his quickly indrawn breath.

Good. He wasn't immune.

She cupped his balls in her palm and rolled them as though they were Chinese baoding balls, handling them gently but firmly.

As she touched him there, she slid her tongue around

the rim of his head, making a full circle before she trailed down his length and back up again. At the top, she enclosed him in her mouth.

As if he were trying to fight his own instinct, he raised his hands *slowly* and buried them in her hair. His fingertips dug into her scalp, urging her to take more.

Lola did, taking his full length, all the way to the back of her throat while twisting her tongue around his girth.

Flannigan pulled himself almost all the way out.

Lola reached out, grabbed his buttocks and brought him back into her.

At first, he moved in and out with an easy rhythm.

Lips stretching, Lola made him go faster, guiding him by flexing her hands and squeezing his tight, sexy ass.

Soon, the firefighter was pumping in and out of her, his head thrown back, his jaw tight.

Yes, this was where she wanted him. Lola willed him to lose all control and come in her mouth.

She brought him close; she could feel it in the way his body tensed. Just a little more, and she'd have him.

At that precise moment, Flannigan pulled free.

Noooo. Lola blinked up at him.

He hooked his hands beneath her arms and stood her on her feet. "You will not make me lose control. Do you hear me?" He gave her arms a little shake.

Her lips curled into a feline smile. "Of course not. You have complete control." She pressed a hand to his chest. "Don't you want to lie down and let me show you just how much control you have?"

He shook his head, his breaths coming in labored pants, like a dog after a challenging run.

Lola schooled her face to keep a triumphant grin from spreading across her face. She gave him a slight push.

He fell onto the bed, his dick protruding from his jeans, his boots still on his feet.

She straddled his leg backward and bent over, giving him full view of her ass and pussy, while she tugged off a boot. Then she stepped over his other thigh and removed the other.

While she was still bent over, a hand smacked her ass, the sound sharper than the pain.

Mmm. She practically purred. "Yes, spank me. I've been a very bad girl."

He smacked her other cheek, a little harder this time.

She turned and straddled both legs, gripped the waistband of his jeans and pulled them over his slim hips and down his magnificent thighs and calves.

He kicked them away with an impatient flick of his legs. Then he scooted back on the bed. "Come here, woman," he commanded.

"As you wish." Lola crawled up his thickly muscled body like a cat playing with its prey. She bent her elbows and dragged her breasts over his cock, pausing long enough to squeeze his length between them.

She skimmed her nipples over his belly, ribs and, finally, to his hard, tattooed chest. "I'm here." She rubbed her sex over the length of his cock before stopping with the tip nudging her entrance. "Your wish is my command."

His eyes narrowed. "Fuck me."

She smiled and leaned back to grab the condom where it lay on the bed beside him. As if she wasn't the one on fire in anticipation of what was to come, she took her time to open the packet, fiddling with the foil until he ripped it from her hands.

In less than a second, he had it open, the condom out and rolled over his enormous dick. By the jerky movements of his hands, his control was unraveling. Then he lifted her by her hips and settled her over his erection. "Now. Fuck me."

She nodded, her quivering body past ready for this final act, the one that would fill the lonely space inside. A place that hadn't been touched since the death of her dearly departed husband of ten beautiful years

Flannigan, the loathsome, cranky, bully of a firefighter, would be her first foray into sex in six years. Six long years without a man to fill that empty space inside.

She sank downward. Once she was fully seated, she slowed her breaths to allow her channel time to adjust to his length and girth.

This was what she'd missed. And the conversation and laughter. She missed so much about her husband. But she'd promised him on his deathbed that she'd move on. Just because he'd had cancer and died, she didn't have to die with him.

And now, she needed to be reminded of how alive she was.

Luckily, Flannigan was doing a damned good job of reminding her.

CHAPTER 4

DANIEL COULDN'T BELIEVE how good Lola felt on top of him and how good he felt inside her. Her pussy gripped him, holding him firmly within. The woman had tight thighs and everything else. She didn't look or feel twelve years older than him.

And what did it matter she was that much older than him? She was right. Older women knew more about pleasing a man than the younger, more naïve ones. How could Chance have missed this little gem? How had he so easily dismissed Lola's obvious charms? All because a few lousy years?

He pumped up into her, loving how she tightened her pelvic muscles, squeezing his dick like nobody's business.

He had to focus on the wall behind her to keep from prematurely ejaculating. God, she had him wound up so tightly, he couldn't think or see straight. All his hot blood raced to his erection, failing to feed his brain so that he could think.

On the very edge of orgasm, he stopped, lifted her up and off him then pushed to his knees.

He flipped Lola onto her stomach, raised her hips and plunged into her from behind.

"Now you're getting the hang of it," Lola said, wriggling her ass for his pleasure.

He thrust in and out, his hands on her hips, slamming her backward against him.

Sensations exploded in and around him. He thrust one last time then bent over her and captured her breasts in his hands. He remained buried in her until the pulsing lessened and his heart resumed its flow of blood to his brain cells.

He eased Lola down to the mattress and rolled them onto their sides, maintaining their connection, his cock still thick and hard inside her. He liked the way she felt encasing him, her bottom pressed to his groin and the backs of her thighs resting against the front of his. Being with Lola was as close to heaven as Daniel could recall ever being.

But he'd be damned if he let her know. She was cocky, too sure of her bedroom skills and would use that knowledge against him in some way, shape or form or another.

He had to make it clear that she should not be calling 911 for non-emergencies. And he needed to make it very clear that Chase Grayson was not the right man for her. His friend didn't even know she existed. Or how good she was in bed, or even how sexy her legs were wrapped around a man's waist. "I need to go."

This time Lola didn't try to delay him. She rolled onto

her back and touched herself down there, where he'd been licking, nibbling and fucking her.

Sweet Jesus, he almost fell getting out of the bed. He had to leave immediately, or risk falling back on top of her and doing it all over again.

After scooping up his clothes, he ran from the room, zipping his jeans. All the way through the house, he could hear Lola chuckle.

She had him, and she knew it.

Well, he'd show her. The next time she called for rescue, he'd ignore the call and let Chance handle it. He would do his job and leave. Grayson wouldn't fall for Lola's sexual innuendos or ridiculous shoes. He'd rescue her from whatever bullshit emergency she cooked up and go on about his business.

Daniel bolted for the front door, still pulling on his boots. When he stepped outside, he straightened, smoothing his hair, and tried to act natural.

Mr. Harden sat on his front porch in a rocking chair. When he spied Daniel, he nodded his head in rhythm with the rocking, a smirk on his face.

Daniel glared. What did the old man know anyway?

He marched to his truck, climbed in, carefully, so as not to hurt his still-hard cock and drove home to a cold shower and an even colder bed. He refused to acknowledge the truth.

Lola Engel had taught him a thing or two about what he really wanted in a woman.

CHAPTER 5

THE FOLLOWING work day at the fire station, Daniel was on edge. Every time a cell phone rang or the station phone clanged overhead, he jumped.

"What's wrong with you, man?" Chance Grayson asked after Daniel nearly knocked him over when he'd spun to answer his cell phone.

"Nothing." Daniel shoved a hand through his hair and tried to calm himself. The shift was nearly over, and Lola hadn't called in an emergency. He'd made it through the day without having to face the challenge. He let go of a sigh. "I'm fine. I just didn't sleep well last night."

"Oh, yeah? Why? Did you have a big date?"

Daniel's head snapped up, and he stared at Chance with narrowed eyes. "Why do you ask?"

Grayson held up his hands. "Just a guess. You're really punchy, like you need to get laid or something." He flashed him a smile. "Well, I'm calling it a day. I have dinner at the ranch tonight with my brothers. I'll see you tomorrow."

The intercom crackled. "We have a woman who needs assistance with a barbeque fire at the following address. Should only need a fire extinguisher to put it out." Erma in dispatch listed the address.

Chance shook his head. "That's the Engel woman's address, isn't it?"

Daniel's heart tripped several beats, and then raced ahead. "No reason for you to miss dinner with your family. I've got this."

Frowning, Chance held up his hand. "No, no. You took it last time. I'll handle it this time."

"No, really. I've got this." Daniel grabbed a fire extinguisher from the storage unit. "I know just what to do."

Chance walked with him out to his truck. "If you're sure…"

"Positive." Fighting back a grin, he slipped into the driver's seat, adjusted his jeans to a more comfortable position over his growing erection and shifted into drive.

He knew just what the woman needed. And he was the man to give it to her.

THE END?

No way! Stay tuned as things heat up between Lola and Daniel in PLAYING WITH FIRE, the next book in the Hellfire Series.

PLAYING WITH FIRE

HELLFIRE BOOK #5

New York Times & USA Today
Bestselling Author

ELLE JAMES

Playing with Fire

A HELLFIRE STORY

ELLE JAMES

NEW YORK TIMES BESTSELLING AUTHOR

CHAPTER 1

"GOT ANOTHER…" Chance Grayson crooked his fingers in mock quotes, "rescue call."

From his position, lying on his back on the weight bench, holding up two-hundred and fifty pounds of dead weight, Daniel Flannigan glanced across at his friend and co-worker. "Lola?" he gritted out.

Chance's lip turned up at one corner. "Who else?"

Daniel settled the weights on the hooks, ducked beneath the bar and sat up. "What's the emergency this time? Cat up a tree? Trapped on top of the roof? Leaf fire out of control?"

Bronson Mattis, the fire chief, strolled into the bay area, catching the tail end of the conversation. "She claims she smells smoke in the attic." The chief looked from Daniel to Chance and back to Daniel. "Who wants to take it?"

Chance held up his hands. "Not me. Flannigan has her number. He knows how to handle her."

The chief's gaze moved to the clock on the wall. "Flannigan, it's yours. Just remember, if a real emergency comes through—"

Daniel nodded. "I know. I'll hightail it to wherever you need me."

"Oh, and just so you know, she requested Grayson." The chief's lips curled in a smirk.

His eyes narrowing, Daniel caught Chance's gaze. "You can take it, if you want."

"No way. She's not for me." Chance yanked his T-shirt over his head. "Besides, it's my turn with the weights."

"Fine." Daniel rose from the bench and dragged his T-shirt over his sweaty torso. "I'll take the call."

"You can take your own truck, and a fire extinguisher, if you think you'll need it," the chief said.

Daniel's groin tightened. Oh, he'd need some way to put out the fire. But it wouldn't be with a fire extinguisher. Hell, he wasn't sure the fire could be put out.

Lola Engel was one hot piece of work. The widow had a thing for Chance Grayson. But Daniel would be damned if the lady would have her way with the Grayson brother. Chance wasn't interested. And all the false calls the woman dreamed up wouldn't make him any more interested.

On the other hand, Daniel found Lola to be...well... incredibly hot. And he didn't mind *responding* to her 911 calls. As long as she knew it was all just for fun, and she kept it that way.

He wasn't interested in a long-term commitment. Been there, done that...had the broken heart to prove it. Falling in love with someone only led to pain. Lola had to know that. She'd been married and lost her husband to cancer.

Back when Daniel worked for US Customs and Border Protection, he'd been in love with his partner. He'd learned a valuable lesson about love during a shootout.

No matter how hard you try, you can't save 'em all. Their orders had been to bring in the coyotes—the people who were hired to sneak illegal aliens across the border—alive. But when they'd surrounded the coyotes, they had gone down shooting. They'd only captured one, injured. The other two had died in the crossfire. And so had Officer Casey Seversen, his partner, and the woman he'd loved. She'd taken a bullet to the groin, just below her bullet-proof vest. That bullet had pierced a main artery. Before they could get her to a medical facility, she'd bled out. Casey had died in his arms. All because of a few Mexican bastards trafficking illegal aliens across the border between Mexico and Texas.

Yeah, Daniel wasn't interested in falling in love again. He'd rather be stabbed in the eye. The pain would be far less.

But a man still had needs...

Did he have a fire extinguisher in the saddlebag of his motorcycle? He unsnapped the saddlebag and looked. Fire extinguisher...Check.

Was there a condom in his wallet? He flipped open his wallet and frowned. Damn. No condoms.

A hand descended on his shoulder. "Need one of these?" Chance's voice sounded behind him, and a condom dropped from the fingers on Daniel's shoulder into the wallet he still held open.

Heat flooded Daniel's cheeks. A man didn't advertise his intentions to get laid. It wasn't cool.

"I was checking for my driver's license." He knew it sounded lame, but whatever. He closed the wallet, with the condom inside. "Don't stay at the station too late. You're expected at the ranch for supper," he said, shifting the focus to Chance and his obligation to show up at the family dinner that evening.

"Hey, you were invited as well. I expect to see you there." Chance's lips curled. "You could bring a guest if you like. I'm sure there will be plenty of food."

Daniel shook his head. What he had with Lola was best kept at Lola's place. Again, he wasn't after a long-term relationship. As long as Lola was okay with that, he'd continue to play her game. "I'll be there. This shouldn't take long."

Chance chuckled. "Nope. It shouldn't take long—if the lady is interested."

"Shut up," Daniel growled. "Who hasn't had a date in months?"

"You," Chance shot back.

Daniel shrugged. "Okay... Who hasn't gotten laid in months?"

Chance's smile slipped. "I could have. There are plenty of women who'd sleep with me."

"Yeah? Then why haven't you gone out with any of them?"

This time, Chance shrugged. "I just haven't been interested in any of them." He frowned. "And we weren't talking about me. We were talking about you and Lola."

"No, we weren't talking about me and Lola. There isn't any 'me and Lola.'" Daniel slung his leg over the seat of his Harley. "I'm not in the market for a clingy woman or anything permanent." He pulled on his helmet and buckled the strap beneath his chin.

"And what makes you think I am?" Chance stared hard at Daniel.

He held his friend's stare for a long moment, and then nodded. "Fair enough. I'll stay out of your business, if you stay out of mine."

Chance held out his hand. "Deal."

Daniel shook the hand then turned the key in the ignition. The cycle's engine roared to life. "Now, if you'll excuse me, I have to check on some smoke."

"Just remember," Chance said. "Where there's smoke, there's fire."

"Yeah," the chief called out, "and if you play with fire, you're likely to get burned."

And Lola was most definitely hot. Even if she was older than him.

As Lola waited for the fire engine to arrive, she checked her reflection in the mirror, patted her hair into place and touched up her lipstick. "Those twenty-somethings don't have anything on me."

And she was right. At forty-three, her abs and ass were as tight as any woman half her age. She spent enough time on her stair-stepper, they ought to be. She turned right then left, admiring how narrow her ankles looked in the Christian Louboutin stiletto pumps she'd just gotten in stock that day. The nude leather with gold piping made her shiver with the kind of excitement only new, expensive shoes and great sex could give her.

Speaking of great sex…

The rumbling of an engine in her driveway made her heart skip several beats. That would be the fire department coming to check on the smoke she'd smelled from the attic. She'd lit a candle up there because it smelled musty, and the stinky sulfur from the matches had given her the idea.

Yes, she called 911 a little too often, but she paid her taxes, and the fire department needed more excuses to get their trucks out. Hellfire hadn't had a fire in weeks. The men needed their exercise.

Just recently, she'd invested in a police scanner that picked up the calls that went out to the sheriff's department as well as the fire station. She refused to call for assistance when the fire department was otherwise occupied for *real* emergencies. Lola timed her calls for the shift when she knew a certain firefighter would be on duty. Chance Grayson was the young man she'd set her sights on. One of the good-looking Grayson brothers who looked so damned desirable in his firefighter uniform.

Instead of the incredibly handsome Chance Grayson, the ruggedly sexy Daniel Flannigan had come to her rescue on more than one occasion. And boy had he known just what buttons to push to make her insides ignite.

Her core heated as she clicked her way through her

home in her fancy heels, anxious to have the firefighter check the attic and what was inside it, including the old sofa she'd painstakingly cleaned to remove a layer of dust. It still had a lot of bounce, and she was ready to test its springs.

A dark silhouette stood framed in the opaque glass of her front door. Schooling her face into a mask of concern, she twisted the knob and braced herself for the rush of excitement.

Daniel Flannigan stood on the other side of the door, a fire extinguisher in his hand, his T-shirt pulled tightly over his broad chest and a sheen of sweat glistening on his suntanned skin.

Lola nearly melted in her expensive stilettoes. She swallowed hard before saying, "I'm so glad you came. I smelled smoke in the attic, and I was afraid there might be an electrical short or something. A girl can't be too careful."

His eyes narrowed, his gaze sweeping over her from the top of her carefully coiffed hair to the tips of her beautiful new shoes. She almost preened but resisted the desire. Her first goal was to get him up into the attic. Then she'd tempt him into testing the springs on the old sofa. Hopefully, nature would take its course and lead to more.

Daniel shook his head. "You have to stop calling 911 for every little thing."

Lola pouted. "Should I wait until the house is completely engulfed in flames before calling? I thought it was prudent to call before it got to that point." She turned away. "Go back to the station. I'll call in a few minutes when my house is almost burned to the ground." Then she walked, model-style across the foyer floor, one foot directly in front of the other, hips swaying, the hem of her skirt barely covering her derriere. She turned just enough to twist her body enticingly. "Unless you want to loan me your fire extinguisher. I can take care of it myself." She held up a hand. "And before you say anything, I have one on order. But until then, there's not a fire extinguisher in this house."

His frown deepened. "You live alone. I would think you'd take all necessary precautions to insure your safety." He glanced at the ceiling. "Do you have fire alarms in every room?"

"For the most part," she said. "I don't have one in the bathrooms." She grinned. "But there is one in my shoe closet."

His eyes widened. "Shoe closet? You have a closet dedicated to shoes?"

"But of course." She enjoyed the look of confusion on his face. "Doesn't every woman need a shoe closet?"

Daniel drew in a deep breath, closed his eyes and shook his head. "Show me to your attic."

"So, now you think there might be merit to my call?" She balanced a fist on one hip.

"Not really, but I won't leave until I've checked it out."

"Humph," she said, but led the way. He was onto her, but she didn't care. He was a male with a fabulous body, and she wasn't wasting another minute they could be making love on the sofa upstairs.

Thankfully, her house was large enough to have real stairs leading up into the top of the house. When her husband had been alive, they'd discussed making a room in the space. But her husband had died, and the idea faded in the dust collecting on the trunks and boxes that had collected over the years in the attic.

She'd spent Sunday, the only day she closed her shoe store, cleaning the dust out of all the nooks and crannies, along with removing boxes full of stuff she didn't need and was finally able to part with. Things that had been her mother's, her mother's mother's and so on.

Some of the boxes contained things Engel had collected from his family. Since her husband had no surviving relatives, and she and Engel had never had children of their own, there was no one to inherit the Engel family photos. Lola hadn't had the heart to get rid of those, even though she didn't know any of the relatives displayed in them and would never look at their images.

As she climbed the stairs, her pulse quickened and the contents of all the remaining boxes faded from her mind.

A hand on her arm made her start. She missed her step on the narrow staircase and would have fallen all the way down if Daniel hadn't been so close that she fell back against his rock-solid chest.

The iron bands of his arms wrapped around her, holding her steady until she could get her stiletto heels back beneath her. His scent surrounded her, one of cologne, sweat and pure male. As she straightened, her knees refused to lock, suddenly feeling like wet noodles. She couldn't make love to him on the staircase. The space was too tight. Lola squared her shoulders and forced her feet to climb the rest of the way up to the attic.

Thankfully, she'd left the door open and the air conditioner from the floor below had cooled the space sufficiently to make it comfortable in the afternoon heat. She sniffed the air and hid a slight smile. It still smelled of the sulfur matches she'd lit, one after the other, in her attempt to make the room smell of smoke.

She'd used the matches to burn some pages from the diary she'd kept while a freshman in college. It was best no one saw the words she'd written confessing to the number of men she'd dated and or slept with. That had been over twenty years ago. Since then, she'd married, had a good husband and lost the man to cancer.

Since Engel's death, she'd gone through several stages of grieving, ending with the conclusion that she couldn't live or dwell in the past. She had the rest of her life to live in the present. That had been when she'd decided she'd gone long enough without male companionship and more importantly...sex.

"I smell sulfur," Daniel said as he climbed the last step and pushed past her into the attic.

Brilliant deduction, Sherlock. The man was a firefighter. What did she expect?

"Is this where you smelled the smoke?" he asked, looking around, the fire extinguisher dangling from his fingertips.

She nodded and turned back to him. "I'm worried it might be an electrical outlet with faulty wiring."

"Do you know where all the outlets are?" he asked, his gaze sweeping the room.

"I suppose," she hedged. When Daniel came to her house, he tended to get straight to the crux of the matter —calling her out on her excessive calls to the department that really didn't require a firefighter to handle. This time, was no different.

Lola could understand his irritation with her wasting his time. But, hell, she'd gone to a lot of trouble to clean the damned attic, she should at least get a chance to have a little fun in it.

She walked around the open space pointing out the electrical sockets and the light fixtures, which took all of two minutes. In the process, she circled the room, stopping in front of the exit.

Daniel showed no signs of his usual…wanting to teach her a *lesson*.

If Lola wanted to take the meeting to the next step, she'd have to do it herself. She unbuttoned the top three buttons of her blouse. "Is it hot in here, or is it just me?" she asked fanning her hand over the cleavage she'd exposed.

"It's hot," he turned to face her. "I don't see any signs of smoke or fire. I think it's safe to say you're not in danger of a fire starting. You might try avoiding striking matches in this space. That would help to eliminate or avoid the scent of sulfur. Now, if you'll excuse me, I'm off duty and headed home."

What? Lola blinked. "You're leaving so soon?"

"Look, Lola, your attic isn't on fire. Next time you call 911, be sure it's an actual emergency. Or…" He shrugged.

Anger flared in Lola's gut. "Or what?" She rounded on him and poked a finger at his chest. "Or you won't come? Well, maybe Chance Grayson will come next time. I'd rather he was the professional firefighter responding to my calls, anyway." She poked him again.

Daniel captured her finger in his big paw. "Ms. Engel—"

"Lola," she said automatically, combatting the heat building low in her belly as she tried to retain her ire in the face of this man's threat.

"Lola," Daniel said, his deep, raspy voice scraping across her skin. "You can't keep crying wolf. One of these days, someone might ignore your call for one they might consider more important." He lifted her finger to his lips and pressed a kiss to the tip. "I'm worried you might end up in a dire situation with no help on the way."

Tingling began in the tip of her finger and spread through her body. She pulled her finger free, not yet ready to give herself over to a seduction. Lola laid her hand on his chest. "Yeah, well, I still think Chance should have come on this call," she muttered, poking his ego rather than his body. She wanted him to work for what came next. Because it would come next. She hadn't worn her Louboutins for nothing.

Daniel slipped an arm around her middle and pulled her close. "You don't want Grayson."

Since he'd moved faster than she'd anticipated, he'd caught her between breaths. "Why not?" she wheezed. Determined to sound more forceful, she drew in a replenishing lungful of air. "He was on the same shift, wasn't he?"

"He was, but he's not your man."

"Neither are you." She lifted her chin. "But you came." She frowned, and her eyes narrowed. "Or did you draw the short straw?" Her cheeks heated. How embarrassing, if he was the one to be stuck with dealing with the crazy widow lady. She struggled to pull free of his arms.

He tipped his head in acknowledgement and tightened his hold around her middle. "I came, because I wanted to. But you should know, you don't have make it an emergency to see me. I have a personal phone. All you have to do is call me. Let me take you out on a date, rather than calling 911."

Her frown pulled her brows lower. "I smelled smoke," she said, her voice less than convincing. Which wasn't exactly a lie. She'd lit the matches that had caused the smoke. And where was the fun in calling the man directly? "Sometimes, a lady needs a hero to storm through her door."

"Is that it?" He grabbed a handful of her blond hair and tilted her head back until she looked straight into his eyes. "You need a hero?"

"Yes," she answered, her voice stronger. "And I don't want to go out on a date. I'm not in the market for a full-time man. I had that."

His hands tightened on her waist. "Then what are you in the market for?"

"I might be older than most of the women you've gone out with, but I still have needs." Holy hell, she was sounding pathetic. And that was the last thing she wanted to be. She shook her head and planted her hands on his chest. "Never mind. I'll take care of my own fire."

"And how will you do that?" He bent and kissed that erogenous zone just below her ear, making her nerves fire on all cylinders. "I'm here." He pulled her earlobe between his teeth and nipped gently. "I have the right equipment."

He nudged her belly with the ridge beneath his fly. "Let me put out the flames."

All the air left Lola's lungs, and her knees turned to goo. She had to slide her arms around his neck or risk sinking to the floor. And once her arms were around the beast's neck, her lips were close enough she couldn't help but brush his stubbled chin. "I want you to know, I'm not in the market for a long-term relationship. My marriage to Engel set the bar too high for anyone to surpass." She found his bottom lip and sucked it between her teeth.

After she let go, he answered, "Good, then we're on the same page. I'm not interested in long-term commitment. It's not what I do."

His voice was a little harsher than she'd expected. Lola leaned back and stared into his eyes, wondering what his story was, but too turned on by what was bumping against her belly to delve deeper into his words and tone. Maybe she'd think about it later. After they tested the springs on the old sofa. "Now that we understand each other…shut up and use your equipment, fireman."

CHAPTER 2

"DANIEL," Kinsey Phillips, Becket Grayson's fiancée greeted him as he entered the kitchen at the Grayson ranch house. "I had almost given up on you. Everyone is out back on the porch. Becket's manning the grill."

"I'd better get out there then and make sure he isn't burning the steaks."

Kinsey chuckled. "You bet. He's notorious for getting distracted. That's why I'm staying inside, finishing up the sides until he's done." She winked and glanced behind him. "What? No date?"

Daniel shook his head. "Who has time to date when you're a firefighter?"

Kinsey snorted in a very unladylike fashion. "Don't give me that. Most firefighters have second jobs because they're off so many days. You could date…if you wanted." She tilted her head to the side, her eyes narrowing. "Hmm. I'll have to see who I can hook you up with."

Daniel raised his hands. "No, thank you. I don't need to be anyone's matchmaking project. I like living alone.

I'm too set in my ways to change now." And he never wanted to go through the kind of pain incurred if you lost the one you loved. Been there, done that, wore the scars.

Kinsey grimaced. "Well, then don't be upset if Phoebe has taken on the role of matchmaker and invited a woman to dinner tonight."

"Phoebe can invite anyone she wants. I don't have to go out with the lady." Daniel frowned. "Do I know her?"

"You know Phoebe…she's Nash's girl." Kinsey winked again. "And yes, you know the woman. A little bird told us that you've been seeing her, even if only on a professional basis."

That had Daniel curious. How many people in Hellfire knew he was seeing a shrink? And why would they invite her to dinner? He hadn't mentioned his visits to Temptation because he knew it would generate questions. So, who knew? And why the hell had they thought he had a thing for his psychiatrist? She wasn't even close to his type.

Kinsey laughed. "You should see your face. I promise, you don't have to hang out with her. There are enough people here for her to talk to, you won't be expected to entertain her." Kinsey shooed him toward the door. "Now, hurry and save the steaks before Becket burns them."

With a deep breath, Daniel stepped out onto the back porch, his gaze taking in the people sitting in rocking chairs, on the porch swing and standing in the yard beside the barbecue grill. Becket manned the spatula, flipping the steaks. Nash stood beside him, handing him a long neck bottle of beer. Phoebe stood with Nash, sipping on a bottle of hard lemonade. Rider Grayson sat in the swing beside the love of his life, Salina Sanchez, who was home on break between semesters from Physicians Assistant school and Chance sat in one of the four rocking chairs enjoying the shade of the porch. Someone else sat in another, on the other side of Chance.

From where Daniel stood in the doorframe, he couldn't see who was on the other side of Chance. He braced himself for a lot of questions and stepped out onto the porch. A foot came into view, and he knew at once who sat in that other rocking chair. And it wasn't his shrink.

Based on the stilettos and their red soles, it could be none other than the woman he'd spent the afternoon with, making the springs squeal on an old sofa in her attic.

Heat rose up his neck and dove south into his groin. On the one hand, he was relieved the woman wasn't his therapist. On the other, their lovemaking was too fresh on his mind.

Lola laughed at something Chance said. Her brown eyes danced with humor, and her smile lit the shadows of the porch awning.

A stab of something hard and new hit him square in the gut.

Phoebe Smith leaned forward on the swing. "Oh, good. Daniel, you made it." She turned to the woman sitting next to Chance. "Lola, you know Daniel Flannigan, don't you?"

Her laughter stopped, and her brow dipped briefly. Then her smile returned, if a little more forced. "Yes, we've met." She nodded her head briefly.

"Did you find the source of the smoke in Lola's attic?"

Chance asked, a wicked grin tugging at the corners of his mouth.

Daniel's lips thinned. "I did." He gave a slight nod in Lola's direction. "She knows how to handle similar situations in the future, right?"

Lola's eyelids lowered, hiding her expression, but the color in her cheeks deepened. "I do."

The scent of grilled steak gave Daniel an excuse to redirect his attention. He descended the steps and joined Becket at the grill. "You gonna burn those? Not everyone likes theirs charbroiled."

"No?" Becket glanced up. "Then hold the tray; I'll pull yours off."

Helping Becket kept Daniel from focusing on Lola and her interaction with Chance. But his ears perked and his pulse quickened every time she laughed.

She'd made it clear from the first call he'd responded to that it was Chance she was targeting for seduction. Daniel had been her consolation prize, though she'd responded to him with enough enthusiasm he was certain he'd satisfied her in every way.

Then why the hell was she flirting with Grayson? A flash of anger made his fists clench.

"Here's the rest of the meat." Kinsey appeared with a tray of raw steaks and chicken breasts. She set them on the table beside the grill and leaned up to kiss Becket. "Is Daniel keeping you straight on how long to cook a steak?"

Becket frowned. "I know how to grill," he growled and hooked an arm around Kinsey's waist, pulling her close to his side.

She nuzzled his neck and whispered in his ear, "Your steak is on fire."

"That's not all that's on fire," he said and kissed her soundly.

Daniel plucked the spatula out of Becket's hand. "Really, man, the steak is on fire." He moved the burning steak out of the flame and over to a less active section of the gas grill. "I'll take over, seeing as you have better things to do," he offered.

Becket didn't argue, but backed away from the grill, continuing to kiss his woman.

"Geez, Becket, get a room," Chance called out from the porch.

"Shut up, Chance." Becket shot a killer look at his younger brother. "You're just jealous you don't have a woman in your life." His brows rose, and he gave a nod toward Lola. "At least, that I know of."

"I like being a bachelor. I don't have to answer to any woman," Chance said. "No offense to you, Lola."

She smiled. "I'm with you. I like my independence."

"Lola, how long were you and Mr. Engel married," Kinsey asked, her expression kind.

"Nineteen years, three months and six days, when he died," she answered softly.

"Wow," Kinsey said. "I'm sorry for your loss. It had to be hard to lose someone you spent more than half of your life with."

Lola nodded. "He was a good man. We had a great marriage. I choose to remember the happiness."

"How long has he been gone?" Phoebe asked.

Lola stared out at the setting sun. "Three years, four

months and two days." She gave a weak smile. "But who's counting?"

The sadness in Lola's voice made Daniel glance up from the grill. She was looking at him, but he guessed she wasn't thinking about him but of her husband.

"You were lucky," Kinsey said. "Not that he died, but that you had it so good while he was here. Some aren't as lucky." She raised a hand to her face and stared off into the distance.

"Hey, babe," Becket dropped a kiss on top of her head. "You're lucky now." He winked. "You have me, and I'll never let anyone hurt you again."

Daniel had heard about Kinsey's ex-boyfriend and how he'd come to Hellfire to reclaim her, considering Kinsey his property. Becket had put a stop to the man's attempt to kidnap and kill Kinsey. Her ex-boyfriend wouldn't bother Kinsey or the Graysons ever again. Now, Kinsey and Becket seemed very happy together.

Daniel dragged his gaze away from the happy couple only to see Phoebe and Nash holding hands on the swing. They, too, had had their challenges in their new relationship, but now they seemed to have worked everything out.

He was surrounded by happy couples, and it made him…twitchy. Like a cat in a room full of rocking chairs.

His gaze went to Lola, who was openly flirting with Chance, smiling and laughing, and not at all worried about the happily-ever-afters surrounding her. Hadn't she said that she'd had her happiness in her first marriage? Why go for second best, when you've had the top shelf your first go-round?

"Can you take this into the dining room?" Kinsey handed him a tray of steaming steaks and chicken breasts.

Becket took the spatula back from Daniel. "I've got this."

Glad for something to do besides stand there and bemoan the fact he was still single and a self-proclaimed happy bachelor, Daniel carried the tray into the house and laid it on a trivet in the middle of the twelve-foot dining room table.

The rest of the guests trailed through the back door, some following Kinsey to the kitchen to help bring out the other food items, including potato salad, baked beans and condiments.

Daniel wanted to grab a seat far enough away from Lola that he wouldn't be tempted to reach beneath the table and touch her. He had his hands on the back of a chair when Kinsey poked her head out of the kitchen. "Daniel, do you mind helping Becket with the last of the food on the grill?"

"Not at all," he answered, though he really didn't want to be last to the table.

By the time he helped Becket with the last heaping tray of steaks and chicken breasts, he was the last person to enter the dining room. Everyone else had claimed seats. Kinsey had the one beside the head of the table where Becket would sit. Nash took the other end with Phoebe by his side. Others had filled the remaining seats, leaving only one chair left. The one between Phoebe and Lola.

Phoebe patted the chair beside her. "I saved this one for you," she said, smiling broadly.

Daniel swallowed a groan and forced a hint of a smile

to his tight lips. "Thanks." He slid into the chair beside Lola, his thigh brushing against hers, the heat it generated making his heart race and his groin tighten. What fresh hell was this? Did the entire town know of their assignations at the end of her 911 calls?

He stared around the table at the covert grins being exchanged. If he wasn't so hungry and the food didn't smell so damned good, he'd get up and walk out. No explanation, no apologies. He'd been the target of the Graysons' matchmaking attempts. They didn't know the score between him and Lola. The relationship was going nowhere. It was just a way for two people to enjoy a little recreational sex. Nothing more.

His thigh brushed against hers again, and an electric shock whipped through him. It didn't matter that Lola was a good ten years older than he was, she had the heart and the body of a much younger woman but the experience and knowledge of what a man liked and what a woman needed from that man. It was a winning combination for friends with benefits. Nothing more.

Her soft hand slipped across his knee, and she leaned close. "Don't sweat it. We both know what they're doing," she whispered. A little louder, she said, "Could you please pass the potato salad?"

Knowing she was as aware of what was going on as he was, he relaxed a little and passed her the bowl of potato salad. Their hands touched, the fire ignited and their gazes locked. For a split second, Daniel was back in the attic, bouncing on the old sofa with Lola beneath him, the springs shrieking with every movement. He'd laughed out

66

loud at the noise, enjoying the sound effects that accompanied their lovemaking.

Lola's lips quirked.

If Daniel wasn't mistaken, she was thinking the same thing.

He'd pass on the steak and beer for another round on that horrendous sofa. And he liked his steak and beer.

LOLA LOVED that Daniel's face mirrored his emotions as he sat surrounded by well-meaning Graysons determined to fix him up with a woman. That they'd chosen her as their experiment made her feel good. Perhaps they didn't see her as an old widow woman, or worse, a cougar on the prowl. In bed, the age difference between her and Daniel didn't mean a thing. Other than she wasn't a shy virgin, or an inexperienced twenty-something. She gave as good as she got when it came to satisfying an itch.

"So, Lola, did you know Daniel worked for US Customs and Border Protection before he came to work at the Hellfire Fire Department?" Chance asked.

Lola paused with her fork full of baked beans halfway to her mouth. "I didn't know that." She turned to Daniel. "What made you change careers? I would think the CBP would be a good job. And the pay has to be a lot better than a small-town fire department can offer."

Daniel's jaw tightened, and he paused before answering. "I needed a change of pace," he muttered, refusing to look up at anyone, probably hoping to end the conversation there.

But Lola was curious. What made a man quit a really

good federal government job to go to work for a city fire department? "I have a friend who flies helicopters for the border patrol on the Canadian border. Where were you assigned?"

Again, he hesitated before answering. "El Paso." Then he shoved a spoonful of potato salad into his mouth.

"I didn't know that." Becket leaned forward. "Were you ever confronted by drug runners or coyotes moving people across the border?"

All eyes turned toward Daniel. He nodded, set his fork beside his plate and looked up, all expression wiped clean from his face. "I was, on a regular basis. It was part of the job."

Lola could hear the tension in his tone. He clenched his fists in his lap. She'd bet his experience with the border patrol hadn't ended well, thus his decision to move to a small town where the excitement was limited to the occasional barbecue grill fire or small grass fire. "Did I see pie in the kitchen?" Lola asked, drawing attention away from Daniel and back to the business of eating a great meal.

Kinsey beamed. "As a matter of fact, there are three pies. Apple, pecan and chocolate cream."

"I'm getting a slice of that apple pie before it's all gone," Becket pushed back from the table and carried his empty plate into the kitchen.

Kinsey hopped up from her seat. "I'll get some dessert plates and forks."

"Let me help," Lola said. She patted Daniel on the leg once and pushed away from the table. After gathering an armload of dishes, she hurried into the kitchen where

Becket was cutting into the apple pie and Kinsey was gathering the dessert plates and silverware.

Lola deposited her load on the counter near the sink and turned. "What can I help you with?"

Kinsey handed her the pecan and the chocolate cream pies. "If you could carry these to the table, I'll get the plates. Becket can carry what's left of the apple pie when he's finished taking half."

"I didn't take half," he called after her. "Only a quarter." He gathered his dessert plate and what was left of the apple pie and followed Lola and Kinsey back into the dining room.

"You weren't kidding about wanting to get your pie before the rest of us." Nash shook his head. "Good thing I like pecan better." He reached for the pecan pie and cut out a slice, placing it on one of the small plates. "Anyone else want pecan pie? I'm slicing."

The pies and plates went around the table.

Lola held up a hand. "I'll pass." She patted her flat belly, proud of how she'd kept the middle-aged bulge at bay. But it was hard, looking at the chocolate cream pie as it slid past her to Daniel. Chocolate cream was her favorite pie.

Daniel sliced a hefty piece and slid it onto a plate. "Sure you won't change your mind?"

Lola swallowed hard to keep from drooling. "I'm sure," she said, her voice weaker, less convincing.

As everyone settled into their pieces of pie, the conversation at the table died down.

With nothing else to do, Lola went back to what had her most curious. "Daniel, how many years did you work for the border patrol?"

He paused with his first forkful of chocolate cream pie and stared across the cream at Lola. "Here, you need this more than I do." He swung the fork toward her.

Automatically, her mouth opened and the pie slid in.

Lola closed her lips around the fork and moaned.

Chuckles erupted around the table.

Lola didn't care. The pie melted on her tongue, an eruption of chocolatey heaven. She moaned again. "So, good," she said around the creamy perfection.

"Nine years," Daniel said. "I was with the border patrol for nine years. Now, can we concentrate on what's important here." He popped a forkful of the pie into his mouth and cut out another for Lola.

She didn't balk, but took the morsel into her mouth and closed her eyes, enjoying it for as long as the creamy deliciousness lasted on her tongue.

"If I'd known that was your favorite," Phoebe said, "I would have made one while I was renting your garage apartment."

Lola swallowed and opened her eyes. Everyone at the table was watching her. Heat crept up her cheeks. "I think it's been three years since I had chocolate pie." She smiled at Phoebe. "Thank you. It was divine."

Everyone at the table laughed, and the conversations continued, with the Grayson brothers poking fun at each other or reminiscing about their younger days. Lola sat next to Daniel, beyond thankful she'd been included in this family's dinner. She hadn't realized how much she'd missed the company of someone else at the table.

"Last bite," Daniel said beside her and thrust the fork in front of her.

Lola took the offering gladly. She'd have to spend an extra hour on the elliptical the next day to burn off the calories she'd ingested, but it was worth every minute of exercise.

She turned to Daniel and smiled. "Thank you for saving me from myself."

"How so?" He scraped the crust crumbs together and mashed them with the fork before popping it in his mouth.

"I wanted the pie, but I knew if I took a piece, I'd eat the whole thing." She sighed. "So, thank you for sharing yours."

He nodded. "Glad to oblige. Besides, it was worth the look of ecstasy on your face." He pushed back from the table and gathered the empty dessert plates.

One by one, the others got up and helped collect items from the table.

"Don't worry about the dishes," Kinsey said. "I'll do those later."

Daniel shook his head. "No way. You invited me and shared your food. The least I can do is the dishes."

"Ditto," Lola said, hopping up from her seat, forgetting she was three inches taller in her stilettoes. She teetered for a second until Daniel reached out with his empty hand and gripped her elbow. "Thanks."

"You should get a good pair of boots," he said. "With flat soles."

"No way," Phoebe said. "Lola's shoes are like a local landmark. I know women who come from all over the state just to shop in her shoe store. Her taste in shoes is part of who she is." Phoebe winked at Lola. "Don't you change a thing. Besides, I love those. Who are you wearing?"

Daniel's brows dipped in a V over his nose. "*Who* are you wearing? They aren't made from human skin, are they?"

Lola and the other ladies in the room all laughed.

"They're Christian Louboutins," Lola said. "I couldn't resist. They make me feel so...so..." She sighed. "It's hard to explain."

"So pretty?" Kinsey said.

"So feminine?" Phoebe added.

"So damn sexy," Chance said and waggled his eyebrows.

Daniel bumped Chance's shoulder and glared.

"What?" Chance raised his hands, his eyes wide. "You two aren't dating or anything, are you?"

Lola patted Chance's arm. "Of course not. I don't date."

"Really?" Chance gave her a calculated glance. "Maybe you haven't met the right man, yet." He straightened, pushing his shoulders back.

Daniel shoved the dishes he was holding into Chance's belly. "On second thoughts, the dishes can wait. You don't mind getting these to the kitchen, do you, Chance?"

"Well, you were on the way..."

"Come with me." Daniel hooked Lola's arm and marched her out the backdoor.

Once out on the deck, Lola grabbed a porch rail and yanked her arm free of his grip. Her heart pounding, she faced Daniel, crossing her arms over her chest. "What the hell was that all about?"

CHAPTER 3

DANIEL SHOVED a hand through his hair and spun to pace the length of the deck and back. He didn't know what had come over him. He had no right to get all possessive with Lola. She didn't belong to him.

Still…seeing Chance hit on her had tweaked his last nerve.

Lola stood with her arms crossed over her rounded breasts, reminding him he'd been kissing those lovely breasts only hours earlier. And also reminding him, any other man could be kissing any part of her. She owed him no exclusivity. The woman had told him she didn't want to date. Nor did she want a long-term commitment.

He stopped in front of her. "You told me you don't want to date. Or is it you don't want to date *me?*"

For a moment she frowned. Then she shook her head. "I told you I didn't want a relationship. Was I not clear on the subject?"

"Yes. Yes, you were," he admitted. He tried not to say it,

but the words blurted out, "Then why were you flirting with Chance?"

A smile tugged at Lola's lips. "Chance is a handsome man. And flirting doesn't mean anything.."

Daniel's gut clenched. "Does Chance know that?"

"That he's handsome?" Lola raised her eyebrows, that soft smile teasing at the corners of her lips.

"No. That flirting, to you, doesn't mean anything. He's young. He might read more into your actions than you intend."

"And you're concerned I might break his heart?" Lola snorted. "You do realize you're not much older than Chance."

"Yeah, but I've seen more action than he ever will. I've experienced more of the bad things life has to offer."

"So, that makes you an expert on flirting and relationships?" Lola shook her head. "Chance is a big boy. I think he can handle anything I throw his way."

Daniel gripped her arms and held her still. "That's just it. I don't want you throwing anything Chance's way." As soon as he said the words, he realized his mistake. But he couldn't take them back, and he didn't want to.

Her eyebrows rose nearly to her hairline. "Really? What part of *I don't want a relationship* do you not understand? You, yourself, said you didn't want a commitment. I had a good marriage. I don't want or need anything long-term. I truly believe nothing can compare. What's your story? Were you dumped by your last girlfriend? Left at the altar? Did she cheat on you?"

Each of Lola's questions drove a knife deeper into Daniel's heart.

"What happened to make you so dead set against love?" Lola's voice had dropped to little more than a whisper.

"She was shot," Daniel blurted. "And I could do nothing to save her." He spun on his booted heel and left the porch, marching away from the house. He would have kept going, but he ran up against the corral fence and stopped.

Anger burned through him. All the emotions he'd felt when Casey had died in his arms resurfaced and stole the breath from his lungs. He stood there for a long moment, struggling to remember how to breathe.

All the time he'd spent with his shrink hadn't gotten him to say those words he'd just spoken to Lola. Hell, he should pay Lola the crazy fees he paid his therapist. She'd gotten him to open up more in one night than anything the psychiatrist had been able to do.

But now that his feelings were out there, where did he go from there?

A slender hand touched his shoulder. Lola didn't say a word. Her fingers trailed down his arm to capture his hand in hers.

For a long moment, they stood staring out at the sky, blanketed in a sparkling display of stars.

Slowly, the anger, guilt and regret seeped from his mind and heart, until he could once again see the beauty of the Texas night sky and smell the scent of Lola's shampoo as she stood close.

"Why did you follow me?" he asked.

"Seems you and I have a lot more in common than just great sex," she said.

"I thought sex was enough." He snorted. "I was wrong."

Her fingers tightened around his, squeezing gently. "Me, too."

"How long does it take for the memories to fade?"

"In my case, I hope they never do," Lola said. "Everything I remember about Engel was good. He helped me become the person I am today. Some days, I miss him so bad, I don't know how I'll go on."

"You were lucky to have had him as long as you did."

"And you?" she asked quietly. "How long did you have her?"

"A year and a half. Casey was my partner. She and I went through a lot before we discovered we were in love."

"She must have been quite the woman to be a border patrol agent," Lola said. She tried to pull her hand free of his, but he held on.

"She was amazing, brave and beautiful." His hand tightened. "She deserved to live, more so than I did. I should have been the one to die that day, not her."

"Unfortunately, we don't get to choose."

"How do you move on?" he asked, his voice absorbed in the dark abyss of night.

"I take it a day at a time and, eventually, it gets easier." She turned to him. "I mean, look at us…we've learned it's okay to have sex." She shrugged. "I'd say that's a step in the right direction."

He lifted her hand and pressed his lips to the backs of her knuckles. "It is."

"Tell you what," Lola said. "If you still want to, let's try the dating thing. We don't have to commit. But it might help us both keep moving in the right direction." She stared up into his eyes, the stars reflecting in her dark orbs. "We might as well." She tipped her head toward the house. "The others think we're already seeing each other —or should be. It might take the monkeys off our backs and keep them from trying to matchmake us with every Tom, Dick—and in your case…Mary." Lola laughed. "I should have seen this coming when Phoebe asked me to dinner. She's been after me to start dating again since she moved out of the garage apartment and in with Nash."

"I didn't see it coming, until I saw you sitting on the porch…next to Chance," Daniel admitted.

Lola glanced down to where her hand laced with his. "Phoebe thinks I'm lonely."

"And are you?" Daniel tipped her chin upward.

She shrugged. "I have a start at being a crazy cat lady. After all, I've chased a kitten up a tree."

He chuckled. "In high-heeled shoes, no less."

A smile flashed across Lola's face. "And you gave me a lecture about wearing those shoes." She tilted her head. "You know I named that cat after you."

His frowned. "You did?"

She nodded. "Flannigan. Only when I'm mad at him, I call him asshat."

Daniel laughed out loud and pulled Lola into his arms. "You say and do the darnedest things."

She wrapped her arms around his waist. "And you keep answering my 911 calls. What does that say about us?"

He shook his head and brushed a kiss across her forehead. "We're both fools?"

"I guess so."

"Does this mean you'll go out on a date with me?" Daniel asked.

Lola sighed. "As long as we remember we're not in this for the long-term."

Daniel held up a hand, Boy Scout style. "I promise not to expect a long-term, happily-ever-after, bonafide relationship. We can even go Dutch, if it makes you feel better."

"Then, yes. I'll go out with you." She held out a hand for him to shake.

"Seriously?" He clucked his tongue. "That'll never do. We've come so much farther than a handshake." He pulled her close, his mouth descending to just within a breath of hers. "I say we seal this bargain with a kiss."

"Deal." Lola lifted on her toes and pressed her lips to his.

When his tongue swept over the seam of her mouth, she opened to him and let him in.

The kiss went well beyond a deal-making peck. Daniel didn't care. It felt right after he'd shared his heartbreak with a woman who'd had heartbreak of her own.

He'd loved Casey with all his heart.

Lola had loved her husband with all her heart.

Was it possible to find love for a second time? If so, would he be able to keep his promise about not expecting a happily-ever-after?

LOLA DROVE HOME that night wondering if she'd made a big mistake. Everything about the evening had been different than she'd expected when she'd agreed to accept

Phoebe's dinner invitation. She hadn't planned on seeing Daniel so soon after rocking the sofa springs with him that afternoon. Perhaps that had been part of the reason she'd agreed to go out with him. She was still glowing in the aftermath of some incredibly passionate sex.

Not that she and her husband hadn't had a good sex life, but they'd been comfortable in the normal positions…in their bed. Never had they ventured outside the bedroom to make love in the kitchen, the living room or the attic.

Daniel seemed content to have her anywhere he could catch her. Up against any wall seemed to suit him just fine.

Lola enjoyed making love to Engel because he'd been her comfort zone, the one who was always there.

Until he wasn't.

With Daniel, every time they came together was anything but comfortable. It was explosive, exhilarating and different from anything she'd had with her husband. Perhaps that was why she'd agreed to date Daniel. Until they had explored all the different ways to make love, she wouldn't be bored of him. And since she'd been so very in love with her husband, she wouldn't be tempted to fall in love with the younger man.

And maybe she could help him get past his own loss.

She glanced in the rearview mirror at the single headlight behind her and smiled, though he couldn't see her.

Daniel had insisted on following her home from the ranch. Never mind it meant he'd have to eat her dust on the gravel ranch road for a quarter of a mile before they reached the pavement of the highway leading into Hellfire. Then he'd have to double back from the way they'd come because he was staying in the hunting cabin on the Graysons' ranch until he found a more permanent home to move into. He hadn't really been trying hard to find a place to live. The cabin suited him fine, and the Graysons weren't complaining about the length of his stay.

A rush of anticipation and adrenaline whisked throughout her body at the possibilities of what could happen once they reached her house in town.

She'd ask if he'd like to join her for a drink. He'd accept.

They wouldn't make it much past closing the front door behind them when the clothes would start flying. They'd make love on her living room couch.

Her pulse pounded by the time she pulled into her driveway.

She got out of her car and fumbled with the key to her house.

Daniel rolled in behind her car on his Harley, looking all badass in black leather and his black helmet.

He didn't get off the bike. Instead, he sat waiting for her to open her door, his bike's engine idling loudly.

Lola frowned. Why wasn't he getting off the bike and walking her up to the door?

When he didn't move from the bike, she called out, "Would you like to come in for a drink?"

He cupped a hand over his helmet where his ear would be, as if to say he couldn't hear her.

Miffed that her plan wasn't quite working out as smoothly as she'd hoped, Lola walked back to where

Daniel sat and repeated her invitation, "Would you like to come in for a drink?"

Daniel removed his helmet and set it on his lap. "Can't. I'm filling in for one of the guys at the station tonight. I'm heading there as soon as you make it safely into your house."

Oh. Well. So much for a quick round of sex-against-the-wall.

Disappointed, Lola turned.

A hand caught hers before she could take a step away. He tugged her against his thigh, cupped the back of her head and kissed her long and hard. "I'll see you tomorrow night for our first date. Wear some shoes you can hike in."

Lola frowned. "Hike? I thought you said date. When do dates include hiking?"

"When they're with me. And pants would be better for riding on the back of the bike."

"Bike?" she squeaked, staring at the one he had his thighs wrapped around. "We could take my car, if you like."

His brows rose. "Are you afraid of riding on a motorcycle?"

She lifted her chin. "Of course not, but—"

"Then I'll see you tomorrow evening at six o'clock sharp. We're going for a ride on my bike. Dress appropriately. I'll bring a spare helmet." Another quick crash of his mouth on hers and he was backing out of the driveway, leaving her too breathless to protest.

He waited at the end of the driveway for her to get into the house and turn on the lights.

Lola fought the urge to run back out and beg him to

come in for a quick late-night snack of kissing and heavy-petting. But she held back, appalled at how much she wanted him.

She'd have to be satisfied that they were going out the next night. She locked the door and turned to her shoe closet with her latest dilemma.

What shoes did she own that she could actually hike in?

CHAPTER 4

DANIEL SPENT the night on duty, but sleeping for the most part. They had one call to check on a man who'd fallen and needed help getting back to his bed. Thankfully for the community...no fires. By late afternoon of the next day, Daniel had worked out with weights twice, run six miles on the treadmill, showered and put on his best pair of blue jeans, a light blue chambray shirt and his hiking boots. He couldn't wait to take Lola to Lookout Mountain to watch the sunset.

He'd called ahead to the diner to have them prepare a takeout bag of roasted chicken, asparagus and baby carrots. For dessert, they would have fudge brownies. He'd make a quick stop at the liquor store where he'd pick up wine and stash it in his motorcycle's saddle bags next to two bottles of frozen water. The water bottles would be nicely refreshing and cool after their hike.

Before he left the bathroom, he splashed on a little cologne and checked his appearance in the mirror. He'd do for first real date with Lola Engel.

As he left the bathroom and passed through the kitchen, the men taking over the next shift looked up from their spaghetti and meatballs.

"Hey, Flannigan, you smell pretty. Got a hot date?" one of the volunteers, Joe Smedley, asked.

Daniel didn't answer. He kept walking.

"I hear you're seeing Widow Engel." The only redhead in the department, Fritz Williams grinned. "Or are you going to fish her cat out of the tree again?"

"What I do when I'm off duty is none of your business," Daniel said.

"Thought so," Fritz nodded, his lips forming a satisfied smirk. "He's going out with Lola."

And thus, the ribbing continued until he'd made it all the way through the room, like running a gauntlet of jabs and gut punches. If he'd thought he could keep his affair with the pretty widow to himself, he'd underestimated the grapevine in a small town the size of Hellfire.

He shrugged off the ribbing and climbed on his motorcycle. Before he could start the engine, his cellphone rang in his pocket. Normally, he let it go to voicemail, but he was concerned it might be Lola, and he didn't want to give her the chance to back out of the date, especially now that the entire town knew.

For the first three rings, he fumbled in his pocket, almost dropped the phone and finally swiped the screen with his finger. "Hey, sweetheart. Don't even think about cancelling our date. I have plans for you."

"Flannigan?" a male voice said into his ear.

Daniel held the cellphone away from his ear just long enough to read the display screen. The call wasn't from

Lola. It was from Roark Stanford, his old supervisor from the CBP. His heart leaped with the joy of hearing from an old friend and then dropped to the bottom of his belly as memories of his last days on the job rushed at him from all sides. He pressed the phone to his ear. "Hey, Stanford. Haven't heard from you in a while. What's happening in the war on the border? How are Jones and Salazar?"

"Jones transferred to Grand Forks, North Dakota. Salazar is still with us. He's expecting another kid."

"How's your wife and daughters? The girls should be heading into high school this year." Daniel sensed his old supervisor had something to say he wasn't going to like hearing. He wasn't sure he wanted to hear what he'd called about.

"Rachel is fine and so are the girls." Stanford continued before Daniel could ask another question, "I called because we might have a situation."

A chill rippled across Daniel's skin. He swallowed hard and braced himself. "Go ahead."

"The Mexican government has a couple missionaries held in one of their jails. These missionaries have connections high up in the political food chain, making them prime candidates for ransom or negotiating bargaining chips."

Daniel's fist tightened around his cellphone. He could think of only one reason Stanford was telling him all about the missionaries and their pull in the US government. Anger boiled deep in his gut. "Please tell me they aren't going to negotiate a trade."

A short pause and Stanford came back on the line. "That's exactly what I'm calling to tell you. I've talked until I'm blue in the face. No one will listen. I've even called my congressmen. He talked to the powers that be, and they wouldn't listen either. Sometime tomorrow they're trading Mateo Villarreal for the missionaries."

He'd known what Stanford would say before he actually voiced the words, but hearing them made a lead weight settle in the pit of Daniel's gut. "You remember what Mateo said at the trial?"

"I do," Stanford replied.

Daniel had been the one to kill Xavier Villarreal, Mateo's brother, after he'd shot Casey. At the trial, Mateo had vowed revenge. "He promised to kill me and anyone close to me."

"I remember his exact words," Stanford said. "That's why I called. The Mexican government promised he won't be allowed back across the border. But you know how empty that promise will be."

Daniel snorted. "Mateo knows all the tricks. He can't be contained or controlled unless he remains locked behind bars in a high-risk penal facility."

"Exactly. I used all those words in my argument, but I might as well have been talking to a wall. They want the missionaries back. And the only trade the Mexican government is willing to consider is Mateo Villarreal."

"Mateo must have someone high up in the Mexican government in his pocket."

"That's what I'm thinking," Stanford said. "Be careful out there."

"Roger," Daniel said and ended the call.

He sat on his bike, staring at Hellfire's Main Street. No

one in town would be safe with Mateo freed. Not as long as he remained in Hellfire.

Then his thoughts went to Lola.

Holy hell.

If Mateo thought for a moment Lola meant anything to Daniel, he'd go after her first. He'd want Daniel to suffer as Mateo had suffered with the loss of his brother.

Now that the town knew he was seeing Lola, leaving wasn't an option. He had to stay and make sure Lola didn't become a target of the rabid coyote. At the same time, he had to distance himself from Lola in hopes the entire town would know he wasn't seeing her, and Mateo wouldn't target her to get back at him for killing Xavier.

Lola would be waiting for him to pick her up and take her out on their date. But he couldn't go through with that plan. Not now that Mateo was about to be released. He pulled out his cellphone and dialed her number. After five rings, her voice came on. "Hi, this is Lola. I'm away from my phone at this time. Please leave a message, and I'll get back to you as soon as possible."

"Lola, I've been thinking..." He took a deep breath, wishing he didn't have to do it, but he knew he had to. "You were right. Neither one of us is ready for commitment, and dating is too much like jumping into a relationship. I won't be over to pick you up tonight, and I think it best if we don't see each other again." He didn't apologize, just ended the call and felt a knife twisting in his belly. He'd really looked forward to taking her out to see the Texas night skies.

Daniel turned his bike away from Lola's house and

toward the sheriff's office. He had to let them know about the shit-storm that was about to hit Hellfire.

LOLA AND HER NEW ASSISTANT, Alma Rosales, had worked hard all day with the new shipment of shoes that had come in that morning. They'd stocked the shelves in the back and rearranged the displays up front and in the windows. By the time five o'clock rolled around, Lola was satisfied with the store and everything in it. And she was ready to get home, shower and change into her best blue jeans and the new hiking boots she'd purchased from the local feed store. They weren't the designer shoes she was used to wearing, but with the right blouse and jeans, they'd be cute, and more importantly, keep her from twisting an ankle on the hike Daniel had promised.

Lola chuckled as she walked the few blocks from her store to her house.

As she passed the fire station, she shot a glance toward the open bay doors, hoping to catch a glimpse of Daniel. Alas, the only firefighter she could see was a shirtless Chance, hosing down the big red firetruck.

She slowed to admire the way his muscles flexed and shone in the afternoon sun. She could admire him without lusting after him like she had BD—Before Daniel. He was a beautiful specimen of maleness, but Daniel...

Daniel was rugged, weathered and bore the external and internal scars of hardship. Something about him called to Lola and made her think of him every waking minute of the day, and much of the night. She shivered in anticipation of seeing him again and making love to him in the starlight.

Chance looked up and waved when he spotted Lola.

She waved back and picked up her pace, anxious to get home and get ready for her evening with Daniel. Their date wouldn't be an emergency call for a quickie. She'd spend time with the man. She wondered if all her talk about avoiding long-term relationships would take a hit after spending an extended length of time with the man.

One date. That was all she'd promised. She'd walk away without asking for, or agreeing to, another. Engel had been her one-and-only. Daniel was a fling. After all, a woman had needs.

She hurried into her house, dropped her purse and cellphone on the counter and shucked clothes as she moved from room to room, making a beeline for the bathroom. In the shower, she washed her hair with the best-smelling shampoo she owned, scrubbed her skin with her loofah, using a body wash guaranteed to drive men wild and paused to tweak her nipples and stroke her sweet spot a little to prime her for what was sure to come later. Oh yeah, she'd been ready for this date since the night before when Daniel had refused to come in for a drink.

The thought of making love on the back of a motor-cycle presented all kinds of challenges. Challenges she would gladly accept. Though younger than Lola, Daniel's rough and ready ability in the bed made her blood heat and her pulse race.

Once out of the shower, she toweled dry and stood naked in front of the mirror, blowing her hair into a fresh style that would be smashed as soon as she slid the helmet over her ears. She sighed as she admired her hair. She'd spent enough money to make sure not even one strand of gray showed. Thankfully, she had her mother's hair. The woman hadn't gone totally gray until well into her seventies. Lola was on track to be the same.

Applying makeup was an art Lola enjoyed. She'd studied online videos on how to make her eyes appear bigger and how to lessen signs of age. Again, she was blessed with good genetics. The wrinkles and crow's feet were minimal, and she kept in good shape through rigorous aerobic exercise, planks, sit ups and lots of hydration.

Hair and makeup...check. Undergarments came next. She had a drawer full of the prettiest bras and panties. With no children to spoil, she liked spoiling herself. Lola went back and forth between black lace and pink satin, finally opting for the pink satin, as it would be more visible in the night. She didn't want Daniel to lose her in the darkness.

Lola chuckled, her heart lighter than it had been since her husband's death. She felt like a giddy teenager preparing for her first date in high school. And she had the perfect outfit to wear over the delicate pink strapless bra and satin panties.

Having scratched the idea of blue jeans, she pulled out black faux leather pants that hugged every inch of the lower half of her body from her hips to her ankles. The matching corset pushed her breasts up, defying gravity and giving her the cleavage she needed to pull off the outfit. She felt like Sandy in *Grease* when she embraced the dark side and showed up at the carnival all in black.

Slinging the matching black, faux-leather jacket over her shoulder, she shoved her key, some money and lipstick into a clutch and grabbed her phone.

Any minute now, she'd hear the deep rumble of his Harley as he rolled into her driveway, all sexy and badass.

She glanced at the clock. Two minutes until six. Her heart pounded, and her breath grew more labored. Lola closed her eyes and strained to hear the sound of Daniel coming up the street.

Her phone pinged the reminder of her date with Daniel.

Lola glanced down at the screen and frowned. Not only was the reminder displaying on the screen, another message showed she'd missed a call.

From Daniel.

Her brow furrowing, Lola touched the screen, unlocking her phone and saw that she'd received a voice mail from Daniel.

She tried to reassure herself he was calling to say he'd been held up because of a raging grass fire, or half of Hellfire was up in flames and he'd be late. But as she listened to the message, her heart sank, and tears welled in her eyes.

He'd had second thoughts.

For a long moment, Lola stared at the phone, her hand trembling. She wanted to strip out of her clothes, scrub the makeup off her face, crawl into her bed and weep.

That was her first inclination. The second rode in on a wave of anger.

Bullshit on second thoughts. She refused to wallow in pity when she looked like a million dollars.

Lola dialed Phoebe's number, praying Nash was at work that evening.

"Hi, Lola, what's up?" Phoebe answered on the first ring.

"Is Nash working the night shift at the sheriff's department?" Lola asked without preamble.

"Yes," Phoebe answered. "Why?"

"I'm in need of a sidekick and a girls' night out. ASAP."

"Really? I was just about to shower and curl up to watch a chick flick. You're welcome to join me."

Lola shook her head. "No. I need noise and movement. Please, come with me to the Ugly Stick Saloon. I'll pick you up and drop you off."

"What's wrong, Lola?" Phoebe asked softly.

"Nothing I can't fix with bourbon on the rocks and a night of dancing with every man in the bar."

"Oh, sweetie, I'll come pick you up. Sounds like you need some alcohol therapy and a designated driver. I'll be there in twenty minutes," Phoebe said. "Don't even think of driving yourself." She ended the call with a click, which left Lola holding the phone, wondering what to do next. Twenty minutes was a lot of time to stand around thinking.

So, she paced. After one circular lap from one end of the living room, through the kitchen and around through the dining room back to the living room, she'd almost tripped twice.

She glanced down at the hiking boots she'd worn

especially for the promised hike to see the Texas stars at night. Boots be damned.

Lola pulled them off, flung them into the corner of the living room and marched into her shoe closet. Her gaze went straight to her Steve Madden rhinestone ankle boots with the four-inch stilettoes. No matter her mood, the boots with all the glittering facets of the rhinestones lifted her spirits. They did this time, too, but only a little.

A little was better than nothing.

She dragged on the ankle boots and stood in front of the mirror, twisting her feet right then left, satisfied she looked hot and dangerous.

"Look out Hellfire and the tri-county area, Lola is on the prowl."

She slipped long rhinestone earrings into her pierced ears and a matching necklace around her throat. A glance at her phone revealed she only had another three minutes to kill before Phoebe arrived.

The rumble of an engine sounded in her driveway, drawing Lola to the window, her heart hammering. Had Daniel changed his mind and decided to come after all?

A car slid into the driveway, and a woman got out.

Lola's heart fell again. She opened the door to find Kinsey standing there, wearing a jean jacket, a flouncy jean skirt with ruffles and a pair of bright red cowboy boots.

"I heard we were having a girls' night out," she said and breezed past Lola into her house. "Where's your liquor cabinet. I'm not driving, and I need a warmup drink." She tossed a glance over her shoulder at Lola. "And it appears you could use one to rev you up to match that outfit. Wowza!"

Lola followed Kinsey into the living room and pointed at the bar in the far corner. "Help yourself, and thanks for coming."

"Us girls have to stick together." Kinsey pulled out two tumblers and poured two fingers of bourbon into each. "Like yours on ice or is straight up good for you?"

"Right now, straight up is what I need."

Kinsey handed her the glass and raised hers in salute. "To kickass outfits and girls' nights out." She upended her glass and downed the clear amber liquid in one long swallow. When she finished, she wiped her mouth with the back of her hand and grinned. "Smooth."

Lola tipped her glass and let the expensive bourbon her husband had loved slide down her throat, warming her insides in seconds.

Before Kinsey could pour another glass, a voice sounded from the door. "Hey, don't start the party without me." Phoebe entered, wearing blue jeans, soft pink cowboy boots and a tight pink sweater that accentuated every curve on her torso. "Let's roll. I need to test the boots Nash bought me...on a dance floor."

Lola fought back a sudden flood of tears. "Are you sure your guys won't mind you going out with me. I'm the only single one amongst us."

"Becket had to stay late at the office. He told me to call if we needed a ride home." She winked at Phoebe. "You're off the hook as the designated driver after we get to the Ugly Stick Saloon."

"Good. I feel the need for a *grande* frozen margarita

with salt. Maybe two." She hooked her arm through Lola's and guided her to the door. "Feel like talking about it?"

"No," Lola said. "I just don't want to be alone tonight. The louder the better."

"Saturday night at the Ugly Stick should be just what the doctor ordered," Kinsey said. "Let's do this."

Surrounded by women who understood her, Lola let them usher her to Phoebe's car and buckle her in. She stared at her house as the Phoebe backed away, wanting to cry. She'd loved the house from the day she and Engel had moved in. They'd renovated every inch of it with love and care. Now that her husband was gone, she'd loved that it contained memories of him in every nook and cranny.

Now, it held memories of Daniel making love to her against the wall, on the couch and in the bed. How was she going to come home to that? Suddenly, the big old house wasn't the haven she'd always thought it was. It was just a big, old, empty house where a lonely widow lived.

Lola squared her shoulders, looked down at her rhinestone ankle boots and refused to give in to self-pity. Tonight, she was out to paint Hellfire red. And if she got lucky, she wouldn't need a ride home with Becket. To hell with Daniel and his second thoughts on dating an older woman.

CHAPTER 5

DANIEL WAS at the sheriff's office, having just explained the situation to Deputy Nash Grayson, when a call came through on Nash's personal cellphone. "That's Phoebe. I'd better get it, since I'm late getting home."

"Yeah, go ahead. I'm about done here, anyway." He turned to leave.

"Wait," Nash held up a finger as he lifted the phone to his ear. "I want a couple more details before you leave. I'll be just a second." He focused on the call. "Hey, Phoebe. Sorry I'm late." He paused, listening.

Daniel didn't like eavesdropping on the man so he moved a few steps away. But he couldn't help overhearing Nash's side of the conversation.

"She did? Girls' night out, huh? You sure you don't need an escort? No? How about a designated driver to get you all home safely at the end of the night?" He shook his head. "No, I don't mind at all. I'd feel better knowing you three weren't drinking and driving. Okay, I'll be on standby for your call when you're ready to come home. Be safe, and don't fall in love with some toothless cowboy." He chuckled. "You have me for that. I love you, too. See ya later." He ended the call and frowned across the room at Daniel. "Something up with Lola?"

Daniel narrowed his eyes, guilt burning a hole in his gut. He hadn't let her down easy. "Why do you ask?"

"Seems the women formed a posse to take Lola out to the Ugly Stick Saloon for a girls' night out."

Daniel's fists clenched, but he managed to shrug nonchalantly. "So? Lola's single and capable of making her own decisions."

"I thought you two were hitting it off, based on what I saw last night at the ranch," Nash said. He slid his cell-phone into his pocket.

Daniel sighed. "I may have broken off a date with her."

Nash winced. "Sounds like she didn't take it well. A girls' night out is a sure sign of that."

"It can't be helped. I had to break it off. If Mateo thinks I have even the slightest feelings for Lola, he'll target her to get back at me. It's best if she's mad at me and would rather spit on me than help me out of bind."

Nash shook his head. "Why didn't you try telling her the truth?"

"She needs to hate me. Mateo is a ruthless killer. He won't hesitate to put a bullet in her heart. Preferably with me watching." Daniel pounded his fist into his palm. "Damn the government for letting him go."

"He might go back to Mexico and stay," Nash offered.

"No way. His last words to me were that he'd find me and kill anyone I cared about, like I killed his brother.

Then he'd kill me." Daniel turned and paced the length of the small office. "I should leave Hellfire."

"And go where?" Nash asked.

"Anywhere to lead Mateo away from here." He spun and faced Nash. "But that can't guarantee he won't find people I've connected with here. You and your brothers have been good to me, making me practically one of the family. Hell, I'm staying on your ranch. He might target the Graysons." He raked a hand through his hair as a hundred awful scenarios blew through his mind.

"We can take care of ourselves, now that we know what we can expect." Nash's lips twisted. "I still think you should tell Lola what's happening. She'll understand and be on the lookout for this Mateo dude."

"I'll tell her, but I still want her to distance herself from me." Daniel's chest squeezed tight. "If anything happens to her because of me…" He couldn't live with himself. He'd lived through Casey's death, blaming himself, taking full responsibility even though it had been Xavier who'd killed her. Daniel should have taken that bullet instead of Casey. He should've let go of Mateo and thrown himself between Xavier and Casey. He'd barely tackled the coyote when Xavier had appeared out of nowhere. Casey had shouted and pointed her weapon at the man, but not before he shot her. Too late to save Casey, Daniel had knocked out Mateo and shot his brother.

"What's your plan?" Nash asked. "You know we'll help you however we can. I'll circulate a BOLO on Mateo and warn all the deputies that he's extremely dangerous."

"Thank you."

"Tomorrow, huh?" Nash shook his head. "We'll be ready."

"I don't think it'll take him long to find his way to Hellfire. He's probably been tracking me from his jail cell, and he knows all the tricks of getting across the border undetected."

"Your friends with the border patrol, will they be looking for him?"

Daniel nodded. "But you and I both know how big the border is. They can't be everywhere."

Nash tipped his head. "Hellfire isn't as big. If they don't grab him coming across, we'll find him here. In the meantime, where can I find you?"

"I'll be at the Ugly Stick Saloon until the ladies leave. I'd offer to drive them home, but that defeats the purpose of putting distance between me and Lola."

"No worries. I'll pull designated driver duties. But by being at the Ugly Stick, won't you just aggravate the situation?"

Daniel's lips pressed into a line. "I don't trust Mateo. He might have some of his cronies in place, waiting for him to arrive and call the shots."

"Understood." Nash held out his hand. "You have friends here. We'll watch your back."

"Thanks." Daniel took the hand and gave it a firm handshake. "I hope no one gets hurt in this situation."

"You and me both."

"Since I'm living on your ranch, that puts you and your loved ones at risk," Daniel reminded him.

"I'll let Kinsey and Phoebe know as well as Nash and

Rider. It's a good thing Mom and Dad are on a cruise. At least we won't have to worry about them."

"You shouldn't have to worry about any of them. It's all my fault for being here."

"You can't blame yourself. Nor can you deal with it alone."

Daniel gave Nash a chin lift. "Thanks." Then he left the sheriff's office, climbed on his motorcycle and headed for the most happening place in the tri-county area. And Saturday night would be crowded. He'd find a dark corner and blend into the background where he could watch out for Lola.

Mateo had friends in high places. He had a network of people on both sides of the border who'd supported his activities, bringing people and drugs into the US. He'd call in all his markers to exact his revenge on Daniel.

"HE STOOD YOU UP?" Phoebe shouted over the music.

Lola took another long swallow of her beer and nodded. "Yup. He didn't even have the nerve to tell me in person. He left a message on my voice mail."

"The bastard," Kinsey said.

"Lemme get this straight," Phoebe's words slurred out long and slow. "He asked you out…and then he left a message, calling off the date?" She shook her head again and swayed. "That makesnooo sense whasssoever."

"Well, it's what happened." No matter how much beer, whiskey or whatever else she'd had, she couldn't get into the spirit of the girls' night out.

"At least you got to bring that outfit to the Ugly Stick."

Phoebe looked around the bar. "You need to get out on the dance floor and show it off. I'd give my eyeteeth for those boots."

"She's right," Kinsey said.

"About the boots?" Lola laughed.

"No, about dancing." Becket's fiancée helped Lola to her feet. "You have to get out there, dance and show that jerk you aren't wasting any tears on his sorry ass."

Lola broke free of Kinsey's hold on her arm. "It's kinda hard to do a two-step by yourself."

"There are plenty of men in this joint. Surely, we can find one to dance with you." Phoebe tapped on the shoulder of a man wearing a cowboy hat. "Excuse me," she said.

The man turned and smiled at her, exposing a mouthful of yellow teeth and some missing out of the set.

"Uh, sorry." She held onto Lola's hand and weaved between the tables, heading for the dance floor in the center of the building. "We'll find someone for you. Jusss you wait."

"Phoebe, you need to sit down before you fall down," Lola said.

"I'm fine."

"We're on a mission," Kinsey said. "There! Deputy Doug." She waved across the room to a nice-looking man with a mustache. "You know Doug Swank, don't you, Lola? Didn't you win him at the last bachelor auction?"

Lola nodded. "I was bidding on the Grayson boys and lost. He was my consolation prize." The man had been nice on a date, but there had been no spark. When the dinner was over, Lola had him take her back to her house.

She'd pecked him on the cheek and never answered his calls afterward.

Kinsey and Phoebe didn't know the history. They were on a mission to see her dance. Lola hoped Doug wouldn't hold a grudge against her and say something ugly in front of her friends. She wasn't sure she could handle a scene. Not after being stood up by the man who made her knees weak and her core ache with longing.

"Doug," Kinsey stopped in front of the deputy and smiled. "You look like a knight in shining armor tonight. How would you like to save a damsel in distress?"

His brow twisted. "I'm sorry, what are you talking about?"

Kinsey stepped back and waved her arm toward Lola. "My friend needs to take her kickass outfit out on the dance floor, but she needs a partner to do it with. Would you be so kind as to dance with her?"

Doug stared over Kinsey's shoulder at Lola.

Heat rose her cheeks, and she started to tell the poor man he didn't have to bother. She could do with another drink, and then maybe head home to await the hangover that was sure to follow.

Surprisingly, Doug smiled at her. "I'd love to dance with your friend." He held out his hand.

Lola hesitated but didn't want to disappoint her friends. She put her hand in Doug's and let him lead her out onto the dance floor that had been recently sprinkled with saw dust.

While she should have been worrying about keeping in step with the deputy, she was wondering if the sawdust would cause any problem with the rhinestones in her boots.

The band struck up a nice slow song perfect for two-stepping. Doug took her hand in his and rested the other around her waist. "It's been a while, hasn't it?"

"I suppose," she said. "I've been so busy with my shop, I haven't had time to think."

Doug's arm tightened around her as he took off in the slow shuffle of a cowboy with a well-seasoned two-step.

Lola had danced with Engel on many occasions, and knew the dance steps so well, she didn't have to think. She moved with the flow of the music and glided around the dance floor, hoping the song would end soon, and with it, the awkwardness of being with someone who clearly liked her but for whom she didn't return the affection.

"You look amazing," Doug said.

She gave him half a smile, not wanting to encourage the man. He was so very nice, but not for her.

Her gaze wandered around the bar, looking for her friends, wishing she was back at their table eating peanuts and drinking another longneck.

In a dark corner of the bar, she could swear she saw a very familiar face.

Doug spun her away from him and back into his arms.

When she looked again, the face she thought she'd seen wasn't there.

Hell, she was seeing Daniel when he wasn't there. What was wrong with her? She'd told him and herself she wasn't going to fall in love again. Engel had been her one and only.

Then why was she so upset that Daniel had stood her

up? She should be thankful he'd seen the light and called it off before they'd gone any further.

She might have fallen for him, and he, being a self-professed bachelor, would have wised up and left her, breaking her heart.

Thankfully, the song came to an end.

Lola smiled at Doug. "Thank you for dancing with me."

"They're playing a waltz. Don't you want to stay for one more dance?" Doug held her hand, refusing to let go.

"I really need to get back to my friends." Lola spotted a lone woman sitting at the edge of the dance floor, her toe tapping to the beat of the waltz. She led Doug over to her. "Do you know how to waltz?"

The woman nodded. "Of course."

"This is Doug." She stepped back and pushed Doug forward. "And you are...?"

"Maggie." The woman smiled up at Doug.

"He's a great dancer, and you look like you'd like to go for a spin." Lola put Maggie's hand in Doug's and beat a hasty retreat.

When she glanced back, Doug and Maggie were waltzing around the dance floor, laughing and smiling.

Lola sighed. At least they were happy.

"Hey, babycakes, why don't you and me trip the light fantastic?" A big hand descended on her shoulder, whirling her around into the arms of a massive cowboy who reeked of stale whiskey and sweat.

"Sorry, I'm leaving," she said and tried to pull free of the man's grip on her shoulder.

"Oh, come on, you can spare one little ol' dance before you leave."

"No," she said firmly. "I can't. Now, let go of me."

His hand left her shoulder.

Lola made a dash for freedom, but a big ham hock of a hand gripped her elbow and dragged her up against the same sweaty body.

"Hey, gorgeous." The man breathed a fog of whiskey into her face, making her want to gag. "Dance with me." He snarled at her. "I insist."

Then she was dragged onto the dance floor and swung into the big smelly guy's arms.

Her first instinct was to stomp the spiked heel of her rhinestone ankle boots into the man's instep. A quick glance at his fat feet encased in thick leather cowboy boots made her think again. Likely, she'd break the heel and ruin her favorite pair of shoes on a lousy drunk. Instead, she looked around the bar, hoping to find Doug. He might be off duty, but he was a sheriff's deputy, and he might flash a badge or something and make the big oaf let her go.

However, Doug was happily dancing with Maggie at the other end of the saw-dusted floor.

If Lola could just lead ham hock hands that direction…

No matter how hard Lola tried to lead the man or break loose, she was stuck dancing with the stinky brute. And if he stepped on her Steve Madden boots one more time, she'd knee the bastard in the groin. Hard.

The man holding her so tightly his fingers would leave prints jerked suddenly and staggered backward, dragging her with him. Then a miracle happened, and he let go to flap his arms to steady himself on his feet.

"George," a familiar male voice said. "I thought the ER doctor told you to lay off the booze."

"Doctor don't know nothin'," George said, frowning at the man who'd pulled him off balance.

Daniel stepped forward. "Wasn't it just last week we were wheeling you into the ER for chest pains and shortness of breath?"

"Yeah, so?" He pressed a hand to his chest as if feeling the same pressure again.

"Didn't the doctor also tell you to follow up with a cardiologist?" Daniel continued, his eyebrows raised.

George shrugged. "Got an appointment for the middle of next week."

"And in the meantime, what were you supposed to do?"

The big guy's shoulders drooped. "Take it easy." He sucked in a breath and stared across at Lola. "But it's Saturday night. Surely I get a day off for good behavior."

Daniel tilted his head. "Maybe I should put a call in now to the guys on duty at the fire station tonight. Thankfully, they're always around when you need them."

George patted his chest, his brow furrowing. "Well, maybe it is time for me to go home."

"What's wrong, George, doesn't your heart know it's your day off?" Daniel asked. "Maybe you'd rather continue dancing with this lovely lady." He turned to Lola and gave her a sly wink.

She shook her head. No way was she going to let George get close enough to grab her arm again. He'd already done enough damage to her body and her ankle boots.

"Nah, I think I'll head home and put my feet up," George said, his hand continuing to press firmly over his heart. "I sure as hell don't want to take another ride in an ambulance."

Daniel patted the man on his back. "Good thinking, George. Maybe you can get a taxi instead of driving your-self home."

"Yeah. You're right. Had a few too many to drive." He wandered back toward his buddies at the table he'd left when he'd captured Lola. Another man nodded and walked with him toward the exit.

"Thank you." Lola rubbed her arm where a fingerprint glowed bright pink.

Daniel frowned in her direction. "Are you all right?"

"I'm fine." She lifted her chin and stared down her nose at him. "I would have gotten away from George on my own. I didn't need your help."

"Okay then, I'll leave you alone." Daniel turned and walked away. No, *I'm sorry I stood you up*. No, *I made a mistake and want to make it up to you*. Nothing.

"Jerk," Lola said out loud and then winced, hoping the music covered her slip of the tongue.

Daniel paused in midstride, but then continued moving forward, without looking back.

Tears clouded Lola's eyes. Shit. He wasn't kidding about not wanting to be with her.

She swallowed hard to keep from crying and turned to find Phoebe and Kinsey standing at the bar, talking to the saloon owner, Audrey Anderson Gray Wolf.

Where had they been when she was being manhandled by George? Lola would have been so much better off if they'd come to her rescue instead of Daniel. Seeing him had only ripped open the alcohol-induced bandage she'd wrapped herself in since arriving at the Ugly Stick.

How was she supposed to get over the man when he showed up in the same places she frequented? She sighed. Hell, the only way to completely avoid him was to move out of Hellfire. And that sure as shit wasn't happening. She had a thriving business, friends and a house. If anyone should leave, it should be Daniel.

Or she'd just have to get over it and move on.

"You look like you could use a friend about now," a male voice said close to her ear.

She turned, hoping to find Daniel had changed his mind and returned to her. The voice didn't sound like Daniel's, but the roar of weekend Ugly Stick Saloon crowd could have distorted it.

Instead of Daniel, she faced Chance Grayson, the man she'd been after for weeks. He held out his hand and drew her into his arms, swaying gently to a cry-in-your-beer kind of song.

Lola leaned against him, finally as close as she'd always wanted to be with the man. But it wasn't what she'd expected.

Yeah, the man was incredibly handsome with rich, reddish brown hair and beautiful blue eyes and lashes any woman would envy. He was well built with rock solid muscles flexing beneath his shirt, and his grip on her body was firm. Her heart should be fluttering, and her pulse should be pounding. But it wasn't. All she could think of was the last time Daniel had held her against a wall and pounded into her like there'd be no tomorrow. And she wanted that.

Damn Daniel to hell.

She looked over Chance's shoulder and caught Daniel looking back at her, his eyes narrowing.

Lola leaned closer to Chance. If Daniel didn't want to date her, why should she care? She never wanted to date a man anyway. And now she had the man she'd been after from the very beginning. Maybe she'd get lucky tonight after all.

CHAPTER 6

DANIEL GRITTED his teeth and stewed in his own juices as he watched Chance clasp Lola in a tight hold and dance her all around the barroom floor. She was close enough her belly was polishing Chance's belt buckle. They might as well be making love on the dance floor.

More than once, Daniel wanted to break them up, just like he'd done with Big George Rhiner. The man had clearly been drunk and straight out of the cow pasture. One whiff of the man's body odor had Daniel feeling sorry for Lola.

And boy, she was hot tonight. As much as he wanted her to wear sensible shoes and save her ankles and legs, the glittering rhinestones on her boots emphasized the sexy black pants, corset and jacket accentuating her luscious curves. Curves he wanted to run his hands all over. Hell, curves he'd planned on making love to that night, had he not received word of Mateo's pending release.

"Let me buy you a beer," a female voice said beside him.

He turned to find Audrey, the bar owner, standing beside him. She wore a sexy tank top with Ugly Stick Saloon emblazoned across her ample breasts. The short, tight jean skirt were the perfect frame to display her long, sexy legs. And the legendary bright red cowboy boots with black studs climbing up the sides completed her gonna-have-fun-tonight look.

Audrey was a looker. Even if Daniel wanted to go after the woman, she was taken. Jackson Gray Wolf, one of the full-blooded Kiowa brothers who lived in Hellfire, had staked his claim years ago. And they had a beautiful baby girl to show for it.

"I could use a drink," he responded, his gaze back on Lola whose hands had climbed up Chance's neck and were laced in the hair at the back of his head.

Daniel's fists clenched.

Chance was his friend. But at that moment, he wanted to plant his fist in the Grayson brother's face.

Audrey caught a blond-haired waitress as she passed by. "Kendall, get this man a bourbon on the rocks."

"Make it a double," he muttered.

Audrey glanced at him, her eyebrows hiked up into her strawberry-blond hair. "Are you driving home tonight?"

Daniel sighed. "I am." He nodded toward Kendall. "Make it a ginger ale." He needed to keep a clear head until they resolved whatever situation Mateo decided to throw their way.

Kendall hurried away, gathering empty glasses and bottles as she weaved between the tables.

"What's got your tighty whiteys in a twist tonight?" Audrey asked. "Anything I can help you with?"

"No," Daniel gritted out. He couldn't take his gaze off Lola in Chance's arms.

"Lola looks great tonight, doesn't she?" Audrey noted.

"I suppose," he responded, reluctantly.

"As much as she loved Engel, I'm happy to see her finally come out of her shell and start living again."

Not only did he have to compete with Chance, but Daniel had to compete with the memory of Lola's dead husband. How exactly did a man compete with a stiff? Not that he was competing. Making a play for Lola was out of the question as long as Mateo Villarreal was on the loose. Which he wasn't…yet.

Although, he *would* be. The very next day.

A chill of apprehension rippled down the back of Daniel's spine. How long would it take Mateo to get back across the border and all the way to Hellfire? A day? Two? A few hours?

Did he even remember Daniel and the part he'd played in the death of his brother Xavier?

Oh, hell yeah. And by all accounts, three years in prison hadn't been nearly enough to cool his heels and let him reflect on his own indiscretions. No, the man was known for his dark heart and penchant for revenge. He'd once tracked a man through the Chihuahuan desert, killed him and all twelve members of his family, including his ten-month-old son and the family dog. He was ruthless and bloodthirsty. He wouldn't stop until he killed Daniel or was himself killed in the process.

Daniel needed to remember to get his handgun out of the gun safe in his cabin. It wouldn't hurt to stock up on rounds as well. Mateo could recruit an army in a short amount of time.

A hand on his arm brought him back to the saloon. "Hey, they're only dancing," Audrey reminded him.

"Some say dancing is foreplay," he said, and immediately regretted letting the words out of his mouth.

Audrey's lips curled into a knowing smile. "It can be. Or in George's case, the prelude to having his junk kneed." She turned her brilliant smile on him. "Thank you for saving Lola from that sloppy drunk. I made sure he was in good hands when he left." She lifted her chin toward Lola. "So, what are you going to do about your attraction to the beautiful widow?"

"Who said I was going to do anything?" Daniel crossed his arms over his chest to hide his clenched fists.

"You're shooting daggers at the Grayson boy. I thought you two were friends and coworkers."

"We were…" Daniel said. "Are," he corrected.

"Well, don't wait too long to state your intentions toward the lady. Or you might lose her to your friend."

"Audrey, you need to know something," Daniel said.

"I need to know a lot of things." Audrey laughed. "What do you have in mind?"

"Be on the lookout for Matteo Villarreal."

"The Mexican coyote they traded for the missionaries?" Her brow furrowed. "I thought they were sending him back to Mexico?"

"They are, but he might try to come here."

Audrey's frown deepened. "Why here?"

He filled her in on why he expected Matteo to show up in the area. When he was done, he added. "If you see him, let the sheriff's department know immediately."

"I will." She touched his arm. "I'm sorry you're having to deal with this. I'll watch out for him." Audrey stared across the barroom toward a tall dark man with black hair and brown-black eyes. She smiled. "Which reminds me...Life is far too short to go without the one you love. Now, if you'll excuse me, I think I need to stack something in the storeroom." The bar owner hurried away toward the hallway at the back of the bar. The tall dark man Daniel knew as Jackson Gray Wolf followed. Before they made it into the shadows, he captured Audrey and kissed her long and hard.

Daniel watched, envying them their love and freedom to express it.

If Lola were his and he wasn't being hunted by a rabid coyote bent on destroying him and everyone he cared about, Daniel might have gone through with that date. He might even have let himself fall in love, despite his protestations about commitment and not wanting to fall in love again.

Lola leaned her head back and laughed at something Chance was saying. The sound was so beautiful it stabbed Daniel square in the chest.

Who was he kidding? He already had it bad for the woman. He just hoped his ruse of breaking it off would keep Mateo from singling her out and making her an example of what he planned to do to Daniel and all the people he cared for.

AFTER TWO DANCES, Lola's feet were killing her. The gorgeous rhinestone ankle boots were meant to walk a short model's runway and then be kicked off for more reasonable and comfortable shoes.

Holy shit. Had she just thought of wearing comfortable shoes? What was the world coming to when the woman with a fetish for fine high heels yearned for comfortable shoes?

"Chance, thank you for dancing with me. I think I'm done for the night."

"Do you need a ride home?" he asked.

"No, I have my friends—" Lola looked around the barroom but couldn't find Phoebe or Kinsey.

Kendall, one of the Ugly Stick Saloon waitresses walked by, carrying a large tray filled with empty mugs, glasses and beer bottles. "Oh, Lola, honey. I have something for you." Expertly shifting the tray onto one shoulder, she reached into her pocket and pulled out a folded napkin. "Phoebe and Kinsey left this for you."

She handed the napkin to Lola and walked away.

Lola frowned down at the napkin, knowing before she unfolded the corners what it was bound to say.

Looked like you were having fun with Chance, and we were tired. Nash picked us up and will be back whenever you call him to take you home. Sorry to duck out on you. Have fun with the rest of your night. Love P and K.

"Did they ditch you?" Chance asked.

Lola nodded. "Sort of. They only came out to humor me out of a foul mood." She glanced around, half-hoping to see Daniel lurking in the shadows, but it appeared he'd left the building. She didn't see him anywhere. Lola sighed. "Don't worry about me, I can call for a taxi."

He touched her arm. "Don't waste your money. I can take you home."

"No," Lola shook her head. "I don't want to bother you."

"I wouldn't have offered if it was a bother. I've had enough noise for the night, too. My ears will be ringing well into the morning." He waved for Kendall, paid his bill and then reached into his pocket for his keys. "Ready?"

"I suppose," she muttered, wondering if Chance was expecting more than just a little conversation on the drive back to Hellfire.

For all the trouble she'd gone to in order to attract this man's attention, now she wasn't so sure she wanted it. No, she was sure. She didn't want anything from Chance but friendship.

Daniel had ruined her for the Grayson brother.

He walked her out to the parking lot and stopped in front of a sleek black motorcycle. "It's not a car or a taxi, but it'll get us where we need to go."

Lola held up her hands. "That's okay. I'd rather call a cab."

Chance chuckled. "Have you never ridden on a motorcycle?"

She shook her head. Daniel was supposed to have taken her out on his that night. And she'd stretched her comfort zone at the idea. But with Chance? He was a known adrenaline junkie. What if he went too fast?

Admit it, she scolded herself. *You wanted your first motorcycle ride to be with Daniel.*

Lola's chest tightened. Daniel hadn't given her the choice to stay together or break it off. Now, she'd never have that first ride with Daniel. It would be with Chance.

"I could call Nash," she said, fumbling in her purse for her cellphone.

"It'll take him another twenty minutes to get here." Chance cocked an eyebrow. "You want to stay that long?"

The sound of the band starting up with the "Cotton-eyed-Joe" sealed the deal. Lola couldn't go back into the saloon and face the drunk cowboys pawing at her and stomping on her beautiful ankle boots.

She looked Chance in the eyes. "You promise not to wreck and scuff my pretty shoes?"

Chance laughed out loud. "What? Your shoes?" He glanced down at the sparkling rhinestones and wiped the smile off his face. Then he held up his hand, scout-style. "I promise to take it slow."

Lola pressed her lips together. "Okay, then. Let's go."

Chance handed her the helmet and helped her adjust the strap beneath her chin. "It's exactly what you needed to complete the outfit. All badass-like." He touched the tip of her nose and flung his leg over the seat. "Hop on and hold on around my waist. When we go into the curves in the road, lean into the turn." He patted the seat behind him.

Taking a deep breath, Lola climbed onto the bike

behind Chance and wrapped her arms around his waist, holding on loosely.

He revved the engine then took off so fast, he almost lost Lola.

She tightened her hold around him and pressed her helmeted head against his back.

As they roared out of the Ugly Stick Saloon parking lot, she felt as if someone was looking at her.

She shot a glance over her shoulder at the bar. Dozens of trucks and cars were parked in the gravel parking lot. One lone figure stood at the entrance, his hands jammed into his pockets, a scowl twisting his face.

Her heart stuttered for a moment, and then her spine stiffened.

Lola snorted and lifted her chin. Daniel had missed his opportunity to take her on her first motorcycle ride. He probably didn't give a rat's ass about who introduced her to motorcycle riding. And she swore she wouldn't let it bother her that he wasn't the one to do it.

She wrapped her arms more firmly around Chance's waist and held on, her breath lodged in her lungs as Chance raced down the highway at breakneck speed.

By the time they reached her house, her hair was a tangled mess beneath the helmet and her arms ached from the death-grip she'd had on Chance.

As soon as he pulled to a stop, Lola slid off sideways and wobbled on her feet.

Chance sucked in a deep breath and laughed. "That's the first breath I've been able to take since you got on."

"Sorry," she said. "I guess I was a little nervous to be on the back of a motorcycle."

"Wow, I can't believe you've gone all your life without riding on a motorcycle." Chance dismounted and stood in front of her.

"My husband wasn't a fan." Lola fumbled with the strap beneath her chin, her hands shaking.

Chance brushed her fingers aside. "Let me." He had the strap through the ring in a second and lifted the helmet off her head. "There. That wasn't so bad, was it?"

She shrugged, afraid she'd hurt his feelings if she told him just how terrified she'd been. "It was all right. Not my preferred mode of travel. I like having heavy metal around me in case of a crash."

"I get that. But one time isn't enough to really know how it is to ride with the engine rumbling between your legs. Say you'll come with me again."

"I don't know," Lola hedged. He was handing her what she'd sworn she'd wanted since she'd seen him shirtless, washing the big red fire truck several months ago. Now, she wasn't certain what she wanted.

Liar.

That pesky voice in her head called her bluff. She wanted Daniel. But he didn't want her.

Chance tipped her chin and stared down at her in the starlight.

Lola braced herself, dreading the moment he would lower his head and press his lips to hers. What was wrong with her? He was a good-looking man. She should be thrilled that a man ten years her junior found her attractive. But he wasn't Daniel.

Chance leaned closer.

Lola edged backward.

He laughed and dropped his hand from her chin. "You like him, don't you?"

"I don't know what you're talking about." She feigned ignorance, rubbing a hand along the arm of her jacket. "Him who?"

"You know who I'm talking about."

"You?" she answered with a question. "You're ten years younger than I am."

"Years don't matter when the heart is involved." He shook his head. "He's crazy about you, as well."

Lola snorted. "I doubt that seriously. Daniel didn't even show up for our date this evening. Besides, we weren't going out with the intention of forming a commitment. We're both happily single. In my case, widowed. I had a good life with my husband. I don't need another man to fill his shoes."

"You wouldn't want another man to fill your husband's shoes. You'd want one who wore his own." Chance gave her a crooked smile. "Daniel is his own person, with his own desires and life goals. He's not anything like Engel, and he wouldn't try to be anyone else."

"I wouldn't want him to be. But I've loved, I've lost and I don't want the heartache of losing the one I care so much about, ever again."

"Your husband wouldn't have wanted you to give up on love. I saw the two of you together. You embraced the joy of life. If you really like Daniel, don't give up on him."

"I don't want a relationship. I just want company. Sometimes." Why did she feel like she'd just told a big fat lie? Her cheeks heated, and she glanced away from Chance's knowing stare.

"If that's the case, I can come by now and then. You know…to keep you company."

Lola's gaze shot back to Chance, her eyes widening. "No, no. That won't be necessary. I've made a nuisance of myself with the fire department already. I must be the butt of the jokes at the station."

"No, but we give Daniel hell about his eagerness to answer your calls."

Warmth stole across her chest. "Eagerness?"

"Yes. Only yesterday, the chief tasked me with responding, but Daniel insisted on being the one." Chance shrugged. "Says to me, he has a thing for you."

Lola's chin sank, and she stared at the shiny facets of her rhinestone boots. "That was yesterday. He's had second thoughts." She looked up and stared into Chance's eyes. "He stood me up, saying it was best if we didn't see each other."

Chance swore beneath his breath. "He's a dumbass."

Tears welled in Lola's eyes. She brushed them away, hoping Chance hadn't seen them. "It doesn't matter. I'm fine by myself." Her words lodged in her throat, sounding garbled at the end.

"Oh, Lola, you don't want to be alone. And Engel wouldn't have wanted you to be alone. Daniel's got to have another reason for such an immediate about face."

Lola swallowed hard, but a sob still rose up her throat and escaped. "I'm sorry. I must be tired. I should go inside." She fumbled with her keys and dropped them on the ground.

"Hey, let me get them." Chance scooped the keys from the ground.

Lola was glad he had. She couldn't have seen them through the lake of tears filling her eyes. "I don't know what's wrong with me. I'm never weepy."

"Come here." He opened his arms.

When she shook her head, he waved his fingers at her. "I promise not to try anything. Just one friend to another. You look like you could use a hug." He raised his eyebrows. "Am I right?"

She shook her head once, thought better and nodded.

Chance pulled her into his arms and held her. Not in a get-in-your-pants kind of way, but in a younger-brother comforting his older sister.

Lola leaned into his strong arms and let the tears slip from her eyes and trail down her cheeks.

Chance was right. She'd needed that hug. If her girl-friends had been there with her, they would have felt much the same. The sound of an engine rumbling down the street didn't even make her glance up.

When it revved and roared away, she broke free of Chance's hold and pushed her hair back from her face to stare at the lone taillight disappearing down the street. "Was that a…"

"Motorcycle?" Chance grinned. "Sure looked like one to me."

Lola frowned. "You think it was…"

"I'd bet my money that was Daniel's Harley. It has an unmistakable rumble." He crossed his arms over his chest and gave her a knowing smile. "That's not the way to his cabin on the ranch."

"He could be going to someone else's house," Lola suggested.

Chance shook his head. "Seriously doubt it. Give him another five minutes. I bet he'll pass by again." Chance slipped his helmet onto his head and buckled up. "Much as I'd like to invite myself in, just to yank his chain, I'd better get back to my place. I'm on duty tomorrow morning. I need some sleep." He chucked her beneath the chin. "If he was worried about you making it home okay, he's not over you. You just have to find out what spooked him and get around it."

Lola shook her head. "I'm not after him for a relationship—"

Chance held up his hand. "We all need to be loved. It's finding the right person that makes it more difficult. Don't give up on him. Daniel's a good guy. He went through a rough patch at his job with the border patrol. He'll come around." He chuckled as he glanced down at his watch. "I'm betting in four minutes." He winked and tipped his head toward Lola's house. "Get inside while I'm watching, and then I'll leave."

Lola gripped the key in her hand, her gaze going to the deserted street. Chance couldn't be right. Daniel didn't want anything to do with her. He'd walked away from her on the dance floor earlier.

After he'd saved her from George's overzealous dance moves.

And he'd driven by her house once. Would he do it again?

Lola hurried to her front door, slipped the key in the lock and turned it. She was inside and locking the door behind her in seconds. She switched on the light but didn't move away from the door.

Chance turned his motorcycle around and pulled out of the driveway, heading in the opposite direction from where Daniel had gone. Out to the ranch where he lived on his days and nights off.

Once Chance was out of sight, Lola turned off the light in the foyer and stared out the long, narrow window at the side of her front door.

A minute passed. Then another. Five minutes crawled by and Daniel had yet to drive back past her house.

She sighed and started to turn away when she heard the muted rumble of a motorcycle engine.

Her heart pounded, and her gaze shot to the street outside. She couldn't see much past the hedges. The glow of a light appeared first. A single headlight like that of a bike or a car with a burned-out bulb.

Lola held her breath and waited, her gaze fixed on the portion of the street she could see from her narrow window.

The motorcycle appeared next, slowing to a crawl in front of her house.

She almost shouted in triumph. Before a sound could escape her lips, she clamped a hand over her mouth and held her breath.

Would he decide to come up the drive and knock on her door to see that she'd made it home in one piece? Or check to see if she'd invited Chance inside? Would he be jealous? He hadn't seemed too pleased to see her dancing with the Grayson brother earlier that evening.

Daniel's motorcycle passed slowly but kept going. Once he'd made it past her driveway, the engine revved and the taillight disappeared.

Well, damn. He wasn't stopping or coming up to the door.

Disappointment flooded Lola's belly.

But the more she thought about what Chance had said, the more hope filled her chest.

Daniel had to care a little, if he'd followed her home to make sure she'd made it there safely.

Lola straightened away from the window, smiling. She was nothing if not determined. And maybe a relationship was what she wanted with the rugged firefighter. The only way she'd find out, was to figure out why he'd backed away, eliminate the obstacle and forge ahead.

Challenge accepted.

CHAPTER 7

Daniel spent the night tossing and turning in the cabin he rented from the Graysons. His plan to push Lola away had worked all too well. He fought between being happy and regretting his decision to break it off.

Seeing her with Chance, the man she'd professed she'd been after from day one, had burned a hole all the way through his gut. How could she go from him to Chance all in the same day?

The answer came as a punch in the belly. Because she really did like Chance more.

Again, Daniel should be glad she'd found the right man for her.

But he wasn't.

She'd be less of a target if she was seen going out with Chance. Mateo might not put two and three together and find out Daniel had been having an affair with the pretty widow.

Mateo.

The man would be free by eight o'clock the following

morning. Traded at the border for the missionaries. They'd come across at the same time as Mateo was escorted back into Mexico.

God, Daniel wished the government wasn't so blind. How could they release a man who'd killed so many people, people who'd only wanted a better life across the border in the US? He was ruthless when delivering the people who paid him to bring them across. Often, he'd left them as soon he'd crossed the Rio Grande, without water or any idea of how to make it to safety.

Daniel had come across some of his victims. One woman had wandered around in circles until she'd passed out from heat exhaustion and died in the scant shade of a prickly pear cactus.

And, though it couldn't be proven, it was rumored Mateo had also been responsible for the deaths of two border patrol officers. They'd been shot in the backs of their heads and left to the buzzards on the border between Laredo and Eagle Pass.

Even when he did fall asleep, Daniel dreamed of the night Casey had been shot. But in his dream, Casey wasn't Casey. She was Lola, dressed all in black leather. She lay on the ground, staring up at him, her eyes vacant.

Daniel had woken with a start and lay still, trying to breathe while his heart raced and his chest constricted.

How was he going to keep anyone safe from Mateo when he didn't know when or if the man would arrive to exact his revenge? Knowing Mateo, he wouldn't come riding into town in full daylight. He'd sneak in at night, like the coyote he was.

By four in the morning, Daniel gave up trying to sleep

and rose from his bed. He pulled on his jeans and boots and a T-shirt. Grabbing his helmet, he got on his bike and headed to the fire station. Since he couldn't sleep, he might as well go to work. He wouldn't be on the clock, but he'd have access to the station's workout equipment. He also kept his good running shoes there. When the sun rose, he could go for a morning run before he went on duty.

And that run might take him by Lola's house. She'd be getting up around that time.

He just wanted to make sure she was safe...and that Chance hadn't circled back after he'd left the night before.

That early in the morning, he didn't pass any traffic on his way into Hellfire. The stars were out in full force, lighting the sky and the road ahead. If all had gone as originally planned the night before, he might still have been lying next to Lola on their picnic blanket beneath those very stars.

Daniel twisted the throttle, forcing the motorcycle to go faster.

He'd pushed her into agreeing to the date in the first place. Then he'd callously called it off in a voicemail. Lola probably thought he was all kinds of jerk. But it had to be that way.

Mateo couldn't know Daniel had feelings for the widow.

Daniel arrived at the station and slipped in the back door, careful not to wake the men sleeping upstairs. At any moment, they could be jerked awake to answer a call from dispatch about a house, barn or grass fire. Or they might have to help someone having medical issues until the EMTs could arrive. Chance had delivered a baby once when the ambulance was on the way to the woman's home on a ranch down a long dirt road.

Daniel had helped deliver the baby of one of the illegal aliens who'd sneaked across the border. The woman had still been damp from her swim across the Rio Grande. He'd been surprised she'd made it as far as she had before going into labor.

At times, he missed his work as a Customs and Border Protection officer. At others, he was glad he wasn't having to deal with all the political issues. Fighting fires was dangerous, but didn't have the same kinds of stress the border patrol dealt with on a daily basis.

Daniel changed into shorts and running shoes. He worked out with weights, did sit-ups and pushups and a variety of calisthenics in the bay with the trucks. When the sun rose, he left the station and ran to the end of Main Street and back, passing Lola's house twice. A light in the upstairs window indicated she was awake. He slowed on his return pass, his gaze on the window.

A shadowy form stood in front of the drawn curtains, silhouetting a slender form.

Daniel came to a complete stop, his pulse continuing to pound as he watched Lola move about the room.

The light blinked out. A few moments later, another light illuminated the living room. Daniel could see through the open blinds of the living room window into the house. Lola stood in the front entrance, dressed in tan slacks and a cream blouse. She grabbed her purse from a hall table and reached for the door handle.

As the door opened, Daniel came to his senses. He

started jogging again, running past Lola's house as fast as he could, without looking back. At the rate he was going, she could have him arrested for stalking, maybe even put out a restraining order to make him cease and desist. And he wouldn't blame her. He was no better than a Peeping Tom, staring through her windows.

He didn't look back until he was a good block and a half away from Lola's. When he did, he was surprised to find her walking in his direction. Until he remembered her shop was another couple of blocks past the station.

Daniel ducked into the station and found a window to look through so he could watch Lola as she walked past. She usually left for her shop later in the morning. Had she found it difficult to sleep as well? A twinge of satisfaction made him glad she was as disturbed by the course of events as he was. He had the urge to run out and explain to her why he'd stood her up.

Lola approached the station on the opposite side of the street.

Even from inside the building, the tap-tap of her heels hitting the concrete sidewalk echoed in the morning air. She didn't turn toward the station but lifted her chin higher as she sailed past.

"Why don't you go after her and make things right?" a voice said from behind him. "You're pretty pathetic, staring after her like a pimple-faced boy afraid to talk to the pretty girl."

"Shut up, Chance," Daniel said, anger burning up his neck into his face. Hadn't the man meddled enough?

"If you're wondering, I didn't sleep with her last night."

Lola disappeared a block later into the local coffee shop.

Daniel turned to face his friend and nemesis. "It's none of my business who you or Ms. Engel sleep with." Though he'd be tempted to punch Grayson in the face if he knew he'd taken her to bed.

"Just putting it out there. She's not interested in me." Chance leaned against the wall, a smile tugging at the corners of his lips. "So, what gives?"

"I don't know what you're talking about."

"The other night at the ranch, you and Lola were getting pretty chummy. We all put money on you going out with her."

"Guess I should have put a bet in that pool." He grabbed a towel from the stack near the weight set and ran it across his sweaty face. "We're not going out. And if you hear anyone say we are, set them straight ASAP."

Something in Daniel's voice made Chance frown. "Seriously, man, what's going on?"

Daniel tossed the towel in the basket they used to collect laundry. "I can't be seen with Lola or any other woman."

Chance shook his head, his frown deepening. "I don't understand."

Daniel paced toward the biggest truck in the bay, spun and marched back. "I should leave. Hellfire and everyone in town are in danger as long as I'm here."

Holding up his hands, Chance said, "Whoa! Back up and tell me what the hell is going on."

Daniel sighed and launched into the story about Mateo. When he was done, he stared at his friend. "That puts you in danger as well. As a friend of mine, Mateo could target you and everyone in your family."

"Damn," Chance shook his head. "We need to have a family powwow as soon as possible."

"Nash already knows. I'm surprised he didn't tell you already."

"I got in late last night and left while he was out tending to the stock." His cellphone buzzed in his pocket. Chance pulled it out and grinned. "Speak of the devil and he calls." He swiped his finger across the screen and hit the speaker button. "Hey, Nash, gotcha on speaker."

"You at the station?" Nash asked.

"I am," Chance said.

"Flannigan with you?" the deputy continued.

"I'm here," Daniel responded.

"I'm watching the news. You might want to tune into the Dallas morning news there at the station. They're making the trade now. It's all about the missionary and his wife. They're not making a big deal about Villarreal."

Daniel cursed and hurried into the station's kitchen and turned on the television.

The guys coming off shift wandered in.

"What's going on?" one asked.

Daniel held up a hand. "Shh."

The news announcer stood in front of the Laredo border crossing. Military vehicles were parked behind him with a couple dozen infantry soldiers outfitted in tactical gear and body armor standing in formation, M4A1 rifles at the ready.

In the middle of the military vehicles was a dark prison transport van. A couple US Marshals dropped down out of the front seat of the van. They opened the side door and helped a man climb down.

Daniel's gut knotted and his fists clenched. "That's him. That's Mateo Villarreal."

Two dark SUVs surrounded by county sheriff patrol cars pulled up and several official-looking men in suits got out. Daniel guessed they were politicians there for the media coverage they'd get out of the show.

The soldiers surrounded the US Marshals, Matteo and the politicians. In a phalanx formation, they moved toward the crossover into Mexico.

The cameraman zoomed in on the other side where a man and a woman were escorted by Mexican officials, police and military personnel.

The two groups met in the middle. The exchange was made, and the cameraman switched his focus to the older missionary couple as they were greeted by their family members.

Daniel couldn't make out what happened with Mateo as the camera view was no longer on the border crossing, but on the movement of the missionaries back into the US.

"What happened to Villarreal?" Daniel reached for the TV remote and switched to another channel covering the same report. The reporter on that station was also covering the reunion of the missionary family.

Nothing in the background gave any indication of where Mateo had gone.

Daniel's heart pinched hard in his chest. "The count-down begins," he whispered softly.

· · ·

LOLA HADN'T SLEPT a wink the night before. Every time she closed her eyes, she saw Daniel stepping in to rescue her from the overgrown, cantankerous drunk, George. He'd handled it beautifully, without instigating a brawl with the big guy. Her dreams also consisted of the erotic variety. She'd made love to Daniel in every room of her house. From the sofa in the attic to the kitchen table. No surface remained untouched by her bare ass. She'd awoken so turned on, she'd had to break out her vibrator to find release.

After that, she'd been awake and unable to go back to sleep.

Instead, she'd risen, dressed and walked to work, showing up a full two hours earlier than usual—and passing the man who'd been the cause of her erotic dreams.

Once she'd arrived at the shop, she'd realized it was Sunday and the store wasn't even open.

Refusing to let that hold her back, she'd worked counting inventory, something she'd put off for long enough. With no customers coming through the door, she was free to spend all of her time doing the administrative task that was part of owning your own store.

So immersed was she in her work and her thoughts, Lola didn't realize the morning was gone and she'd missed lunch until a knock on the front door of her shop made her look up.

Lily Grayson stood outside, a smile on her pretty face, green eyes sparkling and her auburn hair pulled up in a messy bun.

"Lily?" Lola hurried to open the door. "When did you get back?"

"Late last night. Only Becket knew I was coming in. I made him promise not to tell anyone until I'd gotten to sleep all day."

"It's so good to see you." Lola hugged the younger woman. "How was Paris?"

"Beautiful, magical and full of all the latest fashions." Lily hugged herself. "I spent all my off time browsing through stores where I couldn't afford a thing." She grinned. "And the shoes! Oh, Lola, you would have been in heaven over the shoes."

Lola sighed. "I always wanted to go to Paris. Engel and I had planned on going for our twenty-year anniversary." She gave a weak smile. "He didn't make it to the twenty-year mark."

Lily gripped Lola's hands. "You need to go anyway. It was wonderful!"

"Do you think your au pair family will want you to accompany them there next year?"

Lily shrugged. "Maybe. But I like picking different countries. There's a whole world out there to explore."

"And you're being paid while you're exploring. Smart girl." Lola hugged her again. "It is so good that you're home."

"I had to get back and get ready for the new school year."

"Are you still teaching kindergarten at the elementary school?"

"I am. And I can't wait to see all the bright little faces. It's nice to teach, and then send them home. As an au pair,

I tend to work twenty-four-seven, except for the one day a week I get off." She sighed. "But it pays well enough that it's worth it. I get to see the world and come home with money in my pocket."

"I'm glad you came by to see me. But why stop by on Sunday when you know the store's closed."

"I just came from the station. I had to give Chance a hug, or he would have disowned me. When I told them I was going to your place, he and Daniel said they saw you headed this way early this morning and that you hadn't gone home that they knew of."

Lola's heartbeat kicked up a notch. "That was nice of you to stop by the station. I bet Chance was happy to see his little sister. How did they look? Chance and Daniel?" she asked, and regretted the question as soon as she had.

Lily's brow dipped. "Fine. How were they supposed to look?"

"Oh, no different. I just wondered." Heat crept up Lola's neck into her cheeks.

Lily's frown deepened. "Am I missing something? Why the interest in Chance and Daniel?"

"No reason," Lola said. "You need to see my latest shipment of Christian Louboutins. I only got a few, and they'll be gone as soon as the ladies of the community know they're here. But you're lucky, I put them out yesterday before I closed. You're the first one to see them."

Lily's lips curved upward into a crooked smile. "You're avoiding my question. I do want to see the Louboutins, but I'm more interested in the rumors about you and Daniel Flannigan. I also heard through the grapevine you were seen dancing cheek to cheek with my brother Chance. What gives?"

Lola pouted. "And here I thought you were coming to see me and my latest shoe finds." She shook her head. "Gossip. All gossip. There's nothing going on between me and Chance or Daniel."

"Lola, honey. You may be older than I am, but I work with children, and I've become really good at spotting a lie when it's told." Lily raised her eyebrows. "Come on. Fess up."

With a sigh, Lola sank into one of the chairs customers used to try on shoes. "Oh, Lily, I feel like such a teenager when it comes to this dating and relationship thing. I was with my husband for so long, I never really got to date anyone else. I don't know what I'm doing wrong."

"Tell me everything." Lily sank into the seat beside Lola. "I feel like I have a lot of catching up to do."

Lola found herself spilling her guts on everything that had gone on since her friend had left for the summer. She told her about her campaign to win her brother Chance. Her cheeks heated. "I know it was wrong, but your brother is very attractive. And I thought, why not me?" She shrugged. "But it never worked out the way I planned. Daniel Flannigan answered those calls. And I discovered I liked him even better than your brother." She patted Lily's hand. "I know it's hard to think of a woman my age going out with a younger man, but I have needs and desires, too."

"Lola," Lily said. "I think it's wonderful that you're trying to get out there again. I fully understand a woman's needs and wants. As an au pair, I'm discouraged from dating or starting relationships while working with a family. It's too hard to do anything when you're tied up six days out of the week. Sometimes, I just want to be held and hugged by someone other than a tiny person."

Lola laughed softly. "And you're young, with your life in front of you. You should be dating and falling in love."

"I've never thought of you as old. Your spirit and attitude make you blend in with all ages. That's what makes you so good at sales." Lily smiled. "The customers love you. They'd buy gum boots from you just to get to spend time chatting with you."

Lola made a horrified face. "Gum boots? Seriously, Lily, did I not teach you anything when you worked summers for me while you were in high school?"

Lily nodded. "Yes, you did. Gum boots will never be sold in your shoe store."

"Whew," Lola wiped her brow. "You had me worried that Paris didn't take."

"Oh, it took, all right," Lily said. "I'll go back, someday. But not until I've seen more of the world." She touched Lola's arm. "So, what are you going to do about Daniel Flannigan?"

"Not a damned thing."

"From what you've told me, it sounds like he really didn't want to break it off with you."

"I couldn't be mistaken by his message that he wasn't interested in committing to anything at this time." Lola pushed to her feet. "I'm much older than he is. He's just using his logic head. Not the one in his pants."

"But he's not over you. It's obvious by the way he pulled George off you at the Ugly Stick Saloon, and then proceeded to follow you home to make sure you were safe."

"He has a funny way of showing he cares." Lola straightened a shoe that didn't need it then glanced at Lily. "Can we not talk about it? I was just about to wrap up for the day and get something to eat. Care to join me?"

"I wish I could, but the family is having dinner at the house to celebrate my return. I better show up, since the party's for me. I just had to come see my favorite boss, ever." Lily hugged Lola and scanned the shoe displays on the cabinets and the wall. "I'll be back soon to go through all the new items. I have a little money saved back for just such an occasion."

"Don't feel like you have to. I'm sure you have plenty of fashion finds from Paris."

"You have such excellent taste in shoes. I save my shoe shopping for Hellfire." Lily leaned over and kissed Lola's cheek. "It's good to see you."

"And even better to see you, my dear," Lola said. Lily had started to work for her between her sophomore and junior year of high school. Lola had felt like she was the daughter she and Engel had never had. She loved the girl and had connected with her over their love for fine shoes.

Lily headed for the door. "Oh, and remind me to show you the self-defense moves I learned while I was working in Paris. I had a master Krav Maga instructor teach me all about protecting myself. I'm quite good at it."

"I bet you are. Only I don't see a need for it here in Hellfire. Our little town is far quieter than the streets of Paris."

"You never know when you'll need to protect yourself.

I'll be back tomorrow to show you some of those moves. Wear something stretchy and comfortable."

"I have a business to run," Lola protested.

Lily snorted. "You can learn a couple basic moves in less than fifteen minutes. And I can test you periodically throughout the day by dropping in unexpectedly."

"Oh, great. You'll have me on edge all day long, waiting for you to jump out and surprise me. No thanks." Lola laughed. "When did you learn Krav Maga?"

"My employer in Paris wanted his children to stay in shape and learn how to defend themselves. Since I was in charge of them during the day, he had me enroll the children and myself in the Krav Maga program. We spent the summer getting into shape and learning so much about how to defend ourselves. Even Ava, his seven-year-old daughter, could take down her father and escape capture." Lily flexed her arms. "I've never felt better or more in control of my body. It's freeing."

"You should set up an evening training program here in Hellfire. You can do it after your school day ends in the fall and spring. I'm sure there are plenty of women who would love to learn the techniques."

Lily grinned. "That's the plan. I worked up to instructor status in record time. And what better way to give back to the community?" The excitement in her voice was contagious. The teenaged shop assistant who'd come to work for Lola at the tender age of sixteen was now a kickass young woman who traveled to other countries and had a teaching degree.

"I'm so proud of you," Lola said.

"I don't think I would have considered all the possibilities if I hadn't had you as my role model. I'd probably still be in Hellfire, never having been to London, Japan or Paris."

Lola cupped the young woman's cheek. "Adventure is in your blood." She loved Lily so much and was happy she was living life to the fullest. She sighed. "Okay, I'll be your guinea pig. You can show me what you've got."

"Great! Then you can tell me whether you think it would go over well in Hellfire."

"You got it."

"So? How about we start this afternoon? I can come by your house."

"That would be great. Then, if you're not already spoken for, we can have dinner together."

Lily grimaced. "Actually, I am. They're going to have a family dinner tonight to welcome me back."

"That's right. You told me that. I don't know where my mind is. Your family will be thrilled."

"I just wish the folks were here. But they're off on another one of their cruises." Lily shook her head, smiling. "I'm glad they're enjoying their retirement. They both worked so hard on the ranch, they deserve to have fun."

"And now that you're all grown, and Becket has taken over ranching operations, they don't have to be there."

"Exactly." Lily hugged Lola once more and backed toward the door. "I'll see you this afternoon. Will you be home around six?"

Lola nodded. "I'll be ready."

Lily grinned as she opened the front door.

"Hey, is this training going to hurt?" Lola called out.

"It could. But I'll go easy on you to begin with. We'll have to get mats if I open up a training facility."

"Yippee," Lola whispered, feeling the ache in her bones already. "Remember, I'm not twenty-four like you."

Lily wave a hand. "You're never too old to learn how to defend yourself." She grinned. "Besides, you're not old, and you're in great shape."

Her words were a stroke to Lola's ego, but she still wasn't looking forward to whatever torture the younger woman had in mind.

She locked up the shop and walked down Main Street to her house. As she passed the fire station, she saw Lily duck in and hug Chance and Daniel.

Lola sighed. She would like to have been in on that kind of hugging right about now. Going home alone made her feel so empty inside.

Damn Daniel for making everything in her life different, and then leaving her high and dry.

CHAPTER 8

DANIEL PULLED LILY through the fire station door and enveloped her in a bear hug. "Did you do like I asked?"

She nodded. "I got her to agree to some self-defense pointers this evening." Lily planted a hand on her hip and demanded, "Now, are you going to tell me what's going on?"

Daniel exchanged a glance with Chance. "We might have a situation here in Hellfire, and I don't want Lola to get caught in the middle of it. And if she does, I'm hoping your training tips help to keep her safe, in case one of us can't get to her soon enough." He went on to explain about Mateo's vow for vengeance and how he included family and loved ones in his reign of terror.

Lily's eyes widened as she listened. "What does this have to do with Lola?" She glanced between Chance and Daniel. "Mateo is mad at you. As far as I know, you don't have a wife or family in Hellfire. Why would he target Lola?" Her eyes narrowed as she stared into Daniel's eyes. "Unless, there's something going on between you and

Lola." Her face lit in a broad grin. "Is there? Is that what you're afraid of? Wow. I'm gone couple of months and everything changes." She shook head and frowned. "Does Lola know all this? I'm sure she would like to know she's in danger."

Daniel shook his head. "I didn't want to worry her any sooner than I had to. Mateo might not even show up."

Lily crossed her arms over her chest and pressed her lips into a firm line. "I'd want to know, if it were me."

Daniel nodded. "You're right. I'll tell her tonight. I just can't be seen with her, in case Mateo has people watching my every move."

"Do you want me to tell her?" Lily asked. Then she shook her head. "No, it would be better coming from you, since you're the one who dumped her and broke her heart."

"I didn't break her heart. She said she didn't want to start a relationship. She should be happy I backed out of our date."

"Tell me you didn't stand her up?" Lily shook her head. "And *you* asked *her* out?" She whacked his shoulder. "Jerk. All you had to do was tell her what was happening."

"I know I was a jerk. I needed her to think I was a jerk so she'd hate me and no one would think I had feelings for her."

"Ha!" Chance burst out. "So, you admit it." He laughed. "I knew you had it bad for the pretty widow. You looked like you wanted to punch me last night when I was dancing with her." Chance tilted his head. "She's a good dancer, and she's got a great body. I don't know why I didn't notice before."

Daniel punched him in the arm a little more forcefully than a good-natured poke. "Back off."

"Or what? You might have blown your chances with the lady. I can be there to pick up the pieces."

Daniel's fists came up. "Grayson…" he warned.

Chance held up his hands in surrender. "Just saying."

Lily rolled her eyes. "When you two stop acting like teenagers, you might remember Lola is in danger." She frowned. "I don't know how much an hour session in Krav Maga will help. She needs several weeks of it to make it instinctive."

"Anything is better than nothing," Daniel said. "And Nash said he'd have patrols swing by her house more often to keep an eye on her."

Lily crossed her arms over her chest. "Someone needs to move in with her until this is all over."

"Excellent idea," Daniel said. "How do you feel about being Lola's roommate?"

"I could do it, if she agrees to letting me stay."

"But that puts you in danger as well," Chance pointed out.

Lily's eyebrows rose. "My big brother cares?"

Chance frowned. "Of course, I care. When you're not around, who do I have to pick on?" He grabbed her in a neck lock and rubbed his knuckle across her head.

"Cut it out," Lily said.

Chance let her go and grinned. "Haven't done that in more years than I care to remember." He chuckled. "That felt good."

"I swear I'm surrounded by teenagers. My kinder-garten class is more mature than you." She patted her hair back in place, a smile tugging the corners of her lips. "But I can't stay mad at you long." Lily hugged her brother. "I missed you, too."

"As you should."

Daniel envied their sibling banter. As an only child of elderly parents, he didn't have a brother to wrestle with or a sister to pick on or hug when times were rough.

Lily faced Daniel. "So, when are you going to tell her?"

"This evening when I go for a run. I'm on duty until tomorrow morning. I saw her at her shop. She could be there all day. I don't think Mateo will try anything during the daylight and while people are out and about."

"I can pop in every once in a while," Lily said. "I have some work I need to do at the elementary school in preparation for the coming school year, but it shouldn't take me all day."

"Thanks." Daniel shoved a hand through his hair. "Becket's sending Kinsey by, and Nash had Phoebe lined up to visit. This is all assuming Mateo will target Lola. This could be for no reason at all."

"True," Chance agreed. "But I researched the guy. He's bad news. He has no respect for the lives of anyone, even women and children."

Lily frowned. "Why would anyone hire him to get a family across the border?"

"They're desperate," Daniel said. "Their situations are as dangerous, if not more so, where they come from. Some don't have homes to go back to. They're willing to risk everything for a chance at a better life in the US."

"Poor bastards," Lily whispered.

"Look," Daniel said, "I consider the Grayson family my friends."

"We are," Chance agreed. "We've got your back."

"My friendship might put you and yours in danger as well," Daniel warned. "I hope Mateo doesn't come after you."

"Bring it." Lily pushed up her sleeves. "I'm ready."

"Don't get too cocky, Sis," Chance said. "From what I've read, Mateo works in a pack mentality. He doesn't go in alone. No matter how much training you have in Krav Maga, when you're outnumbered, it's a different situation."

"Point taken," Lily said. "We'll just have to make sure we move in packs, too."

"Especially at night," Daniel advised.

Lily nodded. "Right now, I need to head to the school. Think I need a pack to get me there?" She winked.

"You should be all right in the daylight," Chance said.

Daniel nodded. "But avoid shadowy places where people can hide."

"Will do." Lily left the fire station, climbed into her car and headed down Main Street toward the school.

Daniel and Chance stood at the window until her vehicle disappeared.

"God, I hope I'm wrong. I hope Mateo doesn't try to come back across the border."

"You and me both," Chance said, his brow furrowed.

Daniel's cellphone chimed. He pulled it from his back pocket, a knot forming in his belly. The name on the display was Roark Stanford.

He answered on the second ring. "Flannigan here."

"My contacts in Nuevo Laredo say Mateo disappeared an hour after the trade, less than a mile inside the Mexican border and with half of his escort." Stanford pause. "I haven't heard which direction he went, but it might be in your direction. Thought you could use a heads-up."

Daniel's hand tightened around the cellphone. "I appreciate that."

"Keep your head down and be safe," Stanford said,

"Will do." Daniel ended the call and faced Chance. "He's loose as of approximately four hours ago."

"Great. Which gives him enough time to make his way back across the border. He could be well on his way to Hellfire by now." Chance pulled out his phone. "I'll let Nash know. They've already got a BOLO out for Mateo. Any additional information could be helpful."

"And in the meantime, we wait for him to make his move." Daniel bunched his fists. "I'd rather be in a proactive mode than reactive."

"Agreed," Chance said. "But for now, we'll watch and wait."

Daniel stared out the window at Hellfire's quiet Main Street. If Mateo followed through on him promise of vengeance, Hellfire wouldn't be quiet for long.

"We'll do this again tomorrow." Lily lifted her gym bag and slung the strap over her shoulder. "You did really well for a first-timer."

"Thanks." Lola stretched her arms over her head. "I think we worked every muscle in my body. I'll sure feel them tomorrow." She glanced down at the bruises on her arms. "The defensive moves were easier than I thought they would be."

"They're pretty instinctive. After a few more sessions, they'll be second nature."

"Not that I'll have a use for them in a sleepy town like Hellfire," Lola said. "But I go to Dallas often enough, and you never know what you'll run into there."

Lily frowned. "Don't let your guard down, no matter where you are. Hellfire can be just as dangerous. You know, if you ever need company, I could stay over."

Lola laughed. "I appreciate that. But you have your life to live. Staying with an older woman might cramp your style."

"You're not old, and I think of you as a friend and peer." Lily hugged Lola. "I just want you to be safe."

"Honey, I've lived alone now for three years. I've gotten used to it. But thank you for the offer."

Lily gripped Lola's hand. "If you should change your mind, I can be here in minutes."

"Really, I'm fine." Lola frowned. "Why all the concern?"

Lily shrugged. "I don't know. I just have a strange feeling."

"Well, your feeling is creeping me out." She laughed. "You have a life of your own. Go live it."

Lily opened her mouth to say something else. She must have thought better of it because she closed her mouth a smiled. "Okay, then. I'll see you tomorrow for lesson two."

Lola winced and pressed a hand to the small of her back. "I'll be ready...I think."

With a chuckle, Lily left Lola's house and drove toward the Grayson ranch.

Lola stood for a long moment on her front porch, her gaze on Lily as she disappeared at the end of Main Street. About to turn back into her house, Lola caught a movement out of the corner of her eye. She paused with her hand on the doorknob and stared.

The man jogging toward her had dark hair, a bare chest and wore a pair of running shorts.

As he neared, her heart skipped several beats, and then raced ahead.

Daniel.

Lola stared, her hand frozen, her breath catching in her throat. He was less than a block away on the other side of the street when she realized she was gawking like a school girl.

Tearing her gaze from him, she fumbled with the doorknob. When the door opened, she nearly fell into the front foyer and slammed the door shut behind her.

She stood for a moment with her back to the panel, trying to remember how to breathe. Then she ducked sideways to peer through the long narrow window beside the door.

Daniel continued along Main Street, never once glancing her way.

Her heart in her shoes, Lola stepped back from the window, her eyes clouding with tears. Why did she even care?

Because she did. Daniel Flannigan was the first and only man who'd made her feel again after her husband's death. She pressed her palms to her cheeks. "Damn him to hell."

To remind her what a good thing she'd had, Lola walked the hallway, glancing at the photo of her and her husband. They were laughing, smiling and happy.

While Daniel didn't make her want to laugh all the time, he did make her emotions run the gamut of anger, passion and satisfaction. All equally intense. All making her heart pound, reminding her she was still alive, still capable of feeling something for another person.

She pressed her fingers to her lips and touched them to the photo of her and Engel just before he'd passed. He'd been smiling, though he'd been in pain. He'd never wanted to burden her with his illness. As she stared at all the photos, she realized it must have been intimidating for Daniel to make love to her with her dead husband staring at them from the photographs.

Even if Daniel wasn't going to return to her house to make love with her, perhaps it was time to move the old photos into an album.

She plucked several photos from the wall and hugged them to her chest. Like it had been when she'd purged Engel's clothes closet, removing the photos was yet another step in letting go and choosing to move on. She would never forget her husband, or the love they'd shared. He was still the man she measured all others by.

Yet, she realized Daniel couldn't be measured by that standard. They were so completely different.

Lola sighed. It didn't matter. Daniel wanted nothing to do with her. And some of that was her fault for insisting she wasn't interested in a committed relationship. Now that she'd screwed it up, she realized she couldn't be in anything but a committed relationship. It was who she was. When she gave her heart, she gave all of it.

Damn him. Damn her.

Lola trudged toward the kitchen, knowing she needed food to fuel her body, but she wasn't really hungry. She opened the refrigerator door, stared at what was inside, couldn't focus and closed the door again.

She performed the same ritual with the pantry. A scratching sound at the backdoor made her look up.

A face in the window made her scream. Then she realized who it was and pressed a hand to her chest.

"Bastard," she hissed beneath her breath. What was Daniel—the man who'd dumped her—doing at her backdoor in the dark?

"Lola," he called out. "Let me in."

Lola blinked, shaking her head.

"Please, Lola, let me in," he begged.

Against her better judgement, Lola's feet carried her to the door. Her hand hovered over the knob. After he'd stood her up, she was under no obligation to talk to him. He'd explained his reasoning in the voice mail. Had he had a change of heart?

Her pulse quickened. She told herself not to get her hopes up.

There was only one way to find out why he was there.

She opened the back door and stepped back, not wanting her hands, arms or any part of her body to touch his. Knowing how her body reacted to even the smallest of stimuli coming from Daniel, she'd be out of control in seconds.

Daniel stepped through the door, closed it behind him and turned off the kitchen light.

Lola stood still, letting her eyes adjust. "Uh, is there a reason we're standing in the dark?"

"Yes," he said. "I need to talk to you. But I don't want anyone to know I'm here."

So much for Daniel changing his mind. Lola drew in a breath and let it out slowly. "I'm all ears," she said, her tone blunt and cold. She could make out his silhouette and just see the whites of his eyes.

"Can we sit? What I have to tell you will take a few minutes." He reached for her hand.

Lola jerked hers away, turned and led the way to the kitchen table. She sat and waited for him to take the seat across from her.

"I owe you an apology for standing you up last night," he started. "I didn't know what to do. It seemed the only way to get the reaction I needed from you."

"One of complete disdain?" she asked. "You don't owe me anything. You nailed it when you reminded me we weren't in a committed relationship. So, if that's why you here, it's not necessary."

He shook his head in the darkness. "I wish I could see your face, but it has to be this way. I more or less dumped you because I don't want you to get hurt."

Lola laughed out loud. "You dumped me so that I wouldn't get hurt? That's rich." She stopped laughing and stared straight at him. "Don't worry, you didn't hurt me. I'm a big girl. If something isn't working, I don't expect anyone to stick it out."

"That's just it. Too much was working," he said softly.

"I wanted to be with you more than anything, and I can't risk it."

"Please," she said, her voice tight. She was glad for the darkness because it hid the tears welling in her eyes. "You're not making any sense."

"You know I worked for the border patrol, right?"

"Yes. But what does that have to do with you, me and why you pushed me away?"

"One of the men I helped put in jail was released on Sunday."

Still, Lola couldn't see how she was involved, but she let him continue.

"This man's brother killed my partner. I killed his brother in a shootout. In court, he said he would get out of jail, and when he did, he'd come after the me...man who killed his brother."

Lola's breath lodged in her lungs and remained a tight knot as she waited for Daniel to complete his story.

"He also swore he'd make sure that I suffer like he had, by killing anyone I care about."

Lola shook her head. "And he's out of jail?"

Daniel nodded. "They traded him to the Mexican government for a couple of missionaries who had been detained by the Mexican police. Since the handoff, he's disappeared."

The intensity of Daniel's stare made Lola shiver. "When was this?"

He looked up at her. "I learned of the trade Saturday afternoon, just before our date. The trade took place this morning, at the border between Laredo and Nuevo Laredo."

"You knew about it Saturday morning?" she whispered.

He nodded. "I had to put an end to any rumors about us. If Mateo finds out I've been seeing you, and that you mean something to me, he'll target you to get back at me for killing his brother."

Anger boiled up inside Lola. "You should have told me." She pushed back from the table. "Instead, you dumped me like last week's trash."

"I needed you to show your anger and disappointment to the world. Most of Hellfire was already aware of our... times together."

Lola stood and walked away. "So, I'm supposed to thank you?" She spun to face him. "Horseshit."

Daniel stood too. "I didn't know if Mateo still harbored a grudge against me. But I couldn't take the chance he'd show up here. I can't let him hurt you."

"And blowing me off is your way of making sure I don't get hurt." It was a statement, not a question. "That's man-think," Lola said. "And the biggest bunch of horse hooey I've ever heard." She crossed her arms over her chest. "And I'm supposed to forgive you and get over it, because you did it to protect me?"

Daniel shrugged. "I don't expect you'll forgive me. But I want you to know I care. Perhaps too much. If Mateo knows that, you're in danger."

Lola lifted her chin and stared at him in the light shining through the window from the outside porch lamp. "I can take care of myself."

"The little bit of self-defense Lily is teaching you might

not be enough to keep you safe from Mateo. He plays dirty and brings reinforcements."

Lola drew in a deep breath, her anger bubbling over. "And let me guess, you had Lily over here teaching me Krav Maga, not because she's testing her teaching skills in preparation of training all of the women of Hellfire, she's teaching me at your request?" Lola pinched the bridge of her nose. "I must have the biggest sign on my forehead that reads *Sucker.*"

"No, you don't. You're just very trusting." He pushed a hand through his hair. "Look, I'm sorry. I should have told you as soon as I learned anything. I realize that now."

"Yeah, well it's done. You don't have to hang around anymore. I wouldn't want Mateo to see you coming and going from my house. He might get the wrong idea."

"And think we mean something to each other?" Daniel closed the distance between them. "The time away from you is killing me." He stood directly in front of her.

Lola had to tip her head back to look into his face. "You seem fine to me."

He cupped her cheek. "I'm not. I'm worried sick."

She fought the urge to lean into his palm. The warmth of his hand on her face reminded her of all she was missing, too. "I'm mad that you didn't think I was strong enough to handle the news."

"I was wrong."

"I own a gun," she said. It had been her husband's, but she owned it now. She knew how to put the magazine full of bullets into it and how to remove the safety before firing it. Frankly, she was afraid to use it in case the bullet missed the intended target and hit something, or someone else. But Daniel didn't have to know that.

"Where do you keep it?" he asked.

"In my nightstand."

"In a case or loose?"

"What does it matter?" she said. "It's there. I can get to it if I need to."

"If it's not quickly available and ready for use, you might as well not have it." He brushed his thumb across her lip.

A shiver of awareness and longing slipped across Lola's skin. The man made her blood hum, even when she was trying so hard to remain mad at him.

He leaned close, pressing his lips to the side of her neck, just below her earlobe. "How many times have you practiced with it this year?"

"Um…" She couldn't answer when he touched her like that, especially when she rested her hands on his bare chest.

"Once?"

"No," she said, not sure if she was answering him or telling herself. *No, don't fall for his tender tactics.* She suspected it was too late. He had her literally in the palm of his hand. There was no going back. Her anger over his callous omission of the truth only fired her blood, making her burn even hotter. "I'm still mad at you."

"I know." He kissed the tip of her nose. "I don't blame you. Let me make it up to you."

"How?" she whispered, her lips tingling, anticipating his kiss.

"When I'm off duty. Tomorrow night." He lifted her

chin and pressed a gentle kiss on her lips. "I'm afraid if I start now, I won't stop."

"Then don't."

"I'm actually on the job, just out for a little exercise."

"Sex can be counted as exercise," she said, rising on her toes to press her mouth to his.

"I would, if I was getting off duty now, but I'm on duty until seven o'clock tomorrow morning." He leaned his forehead against hers. "Do you want me to get someone to stay the night with you?"

She shook her head. "Not unless it's you."

"The sheriff's department drive by as often as the can."

"And I'll get my gun out of my case and put it on the night stand," she promised.

"Just be careful and don't hurt yourself."

Lola laughed. "Tell Lily that. I have bruises all over from our first self-defense training session. That girl is fierce."

He brushed his lips across hers again and sighed. "I have to go."

"Will you be all right out there? It's dark now. What if Mateo is lying in wait for you?" Lola wrapped her arms around his waist and squeezed hard. "He might come after me, but he's probably more likely to hurt you. Please, be careful."

"I will. Call me later, before you go to sleep. Let me know you're all right. And if you have a security system in this old house...use it."

She grimaced. "I don't. I never needed one until now."

Daniel frowned and walked to the back door. "Lock

this behind me, and doublecheck every door and window in the house to make sure they are secure."

"Yes, sir," she said.

"I'll call later." And Daniel was gone, slipping into the shadows of darkness.

Lola locked the back door and stared through the window. Then she ran to the front of the house and watched as he emerged onto Main Street, several houses down. From there, he jogged back to the fire station.

Anger warred with joy and unease.

He hadn't told her about the threat, but he'd done it because he cared and didn't want Mateo to know he cared about her. The thought of Mateo running free with the potential of showing up in Hellfire made her blood chill. She wasn't as worried about herself as much as she was about Daniel. Mateo sounded like a really bad dude. How would she be able to help Daniel stay safe? He'd probably say by staying safe herself. If Mateo got hold of her, he could use her to draw Daniel out. Daniel would come.

Because he cared. Warmth spread across her chest and quickly faded.

Then Mateo would kill her and Daniel.

CHAPTER 9

MONDAY WAS a typical day at the shoe store. Or so it should have been. For the most part, her days usually consisted of helping ladies choose the right shoe for them and stocking shelves, ordering more shoes and deciding what to fix for dinner. The only difference for this overcast Monday was that she and Daniel might be the targets of Mateo Villarreal, a ruthless coyote bent on revenge. That wasn't something she usually had to contend with in the normal course of her day.

Thankfully, working helped keep her occupied so she didn't have time to worry.

With the recent arrival of new stock, Lola got busy notifying her customers. Soon, she and Alma were assisting ladies with different sizes and styles. Not until two o'clock did they have enough of a break between customers to eat lunch.

All day long, Lola sensed that Alma was nervous as well. But she couldn't decide if it was because Lola was emitting worry pheromones or Alma had something else bothering her.

"You can take your lunchbreak first," Lola said, as soon as they had a lull between customers.

Alma nodded. "Thanks. I want to check on my mother. She isn't feeling well."

"I'm sorry. Let her know I'm thinking about her. If you need to stay home, I can handle the rest of the day by myself." And she preferred Alma to be gone before closing time. If Mateo was watching her, he'd wait until the store emptied of customers before he made his move. At least, that was how Lola would do it. Not that she was a ruthless killer or anything, but she was current on her TV crime dramas.

Alma glanced out the window before looking back at Lola. "I think I will stay home with her." She grabbed her purse and headed for the front door. When she reached for the handle, she paused and looked back over her shoulder. "You should go home, too. There's only another hour before the store closes, and there aren't any customers."

Lola frowned. "I always stay open until five-thirty for the ladies getting off work to have a chance to drop by before going home. With this new shipment, I don't want to disappoint them."

Alma chewed on her bottom lip. "Maybe I should stay. You might need help."

"Since your mother isn't feeling well, you should be with her." Lola crossed to Alma and smiled at her. "I can handle the store on my own."

Still Alma hesitated.

"What's wrong, Alma?" Lola touched the pretty, young Hispanic woman's arm. "You've been jumpy all day."

Alma looked down, refusing to meet Lola's gaze. She fiddled with her purse strap and finally blurted out, "You're in danger, Ms. Lola."

Lola wasn't expecting Alma to know of her troubles. "How do you know this?"

Alma looked away. "I can't say."

Lola wanted to grab the woman and shake the information out of her. She held back her frustration and spoke softly, "It's okay. Whatever you have to say, I won't tell a soul I heard it from you."

Alma shook her head, tears welling in her eyes. "There are people in the barrio where I live. They're afraid."

"Of what?" Lola asked. "Or who?" She gripped Alma's arms and pulled her deeper into the store, away from the front windows. "Alma, are they threatening you? Do you need a safe place to stay?"

Alma shook her head. "I must go home. I can't leave my mother."

"Perhaps I need to close up shop so that we can drive over to your place and pick up your mother. We could take the two of you to a safe place until the trouble blows over." She wasn't sure where that would be, but she'd find someplace, dammit. She'd offer her house, but from what Daniel said, anywhere near Lola and Daniel wasn't safe.

Tears spilled down Alma's cheeks. "There are people in the barrio who are in the US illegally. They have everything to lose if they are caught."

"Who would catch them?" Lola asked. "Are you afraid the sheriff's department will raid them?"

"No," Alma smiled. "They don't usually get involved in immigration issues."

"Are you afraid of ICE, Immigration and Customs Enforcement?"

Alma shook her head. "No. The people in the barrio are afraid of the people who brought them across the border. If they don't do as they are told, they could be killed and their bodies tossed in the desert."

"Sweet Jesus," Lola said softly. She pulled Alma into her arms. "Seriously, let me get you and your mother out of there. I'll take you somewhere safe."

"No." Alma stepped away. "You can't go near the barrio."

"Alma," Lola looked straight into Alma's eyes. "Is Mateo Villarreal in town?"

The Hispanic woman's dark face paled. "I can't say."

"Sweetie, you can't go back to the barrio."

"I have to," she whispered. "I can't leave my mother."

"Then I'll send one of the sheriff's deputies to get her." Lola gripped Alma's arms. "I wish you had said something earlier. You know you can trust me."

"I trust you with my life. It's others I don't trust with my mother's life." She pushed Lola's hands from her arms. "I have to go home. If I don't, they will know I told you something. Just, please…stay safe. Leave town. Go to Dallas. Get out of Hellfire."

"Alma, this is my home."

"Please, Ms. Lola. I beg you," she cried, tears flowing down her face. "Please leave."

"I'll consider it," she said to appease the woman. She had no intention of leaving Hellfire. Everything she knew and loved was in this little town. Some badass, human-trafficking criminal was not going to scare her away. And she wouldn't leave, knowing Daniel was also in danger.

"I must go." Alma hurried toward the door.

"Be safe, Alma. If all is well, I'll see you tomorrow for work." She gave the woman a weak smile. Her gut told her things were about to get worse before they got better. An image of Engel's pistol flashed through her mind. She'd tucked it into the drawer of her nightstand. She'd put it under her pillow tonight before she laid down to sleep. Lola was beginning to wonder whether she should swing by the shelter and adopt a dog. A very big dog.

Lola watched until Alma climbed into her secondhand older model car and drove away. She worried about the young woman and her mother.

A sound behind her alerted her to the fact she wasn't alone, seconds before arms wrapped around her throat.

Lola cupped the arms with her hands and ducked beneath her attacker's elbow and shouted, "Back off!" She spun and faced her attacker, her foot halfway up in a kick to the groin when she recognized the man.

"Whoa." Rider Grayson jumped back, avoiding the heel aimed for his groin. "I wasn't expecting that."

Clapping sounded behind him. Lily stepped up beside her brother, grinning. "Very good. Your lesson took."

Lola pressed a hand to her pounding chest. "You scared the bejeezus out of me," she said, her voice ragged as she tried to catch her breath.

"I wanted to see if you were ready for anything," Lily said. "Rider volunteered to test you."

Rider Grayson held up his hands. "It was Lily's idea. I

wouldn't have gone along with it had I known I could have been permanently scarred." He winked. "By the way, good move."

Lola shook her head. "I hope I don't have to use it for real."

"But if you do, you're ready," Lily said. "I'm coming over this afternoon to show you some more moves. Want me to pack a bag?"

Lola shot the young woman a mild glare. "You could have told me what was happening instead of making me think you were only practicing for your own training class."

"I didn't think it was my place. And Daniel said he was going to tell you yesterday evening. I figured since he stood you up for your date, he should be the one to apologize and fill you in." Lily grimaced. "Sorry. But now that you know, we have to make sure you have enough moves to keep you safe. And that offer still stands for me to move in with you until this situation is resolved. Do you forgive me?" Lily gave her a hopeful smile.

"You're forgiven," Lola said, grudgingly.

"How about Daniel?" Lily asked.

"I'm still mad at him," she said, though her anger didn't come out in her voice. Not after that kiss the night before. Heat soared through her veins, pooling south at her core. Then she remembered where she was. The heat that had gone south rushed north into her cheeks. "What were we talking about?"

Lily laughed. "Uh huh. Still mad?" She shook her head. "I'll be by in an hour. Rider said he would escort you home."

"I don't need an escort," Lola nodded toward the window. "It's still light outside. I only have to walk down Main Street. I'll be fine."

"If it's all the same to you, I'd like to walk you home," Rider said. "My shop is only a block further. Besides, Salina would be mad at me if I didn't walk you home."

"Salina knows what's going on?" Lola asked.

"All the Graysons know," Lily said. "We've got your back."

"If Salina was here, she'd walk you herself," Rider said.

"How's she doing in PA school?" Lola asked.

"Great. She has a break coming up soon. We're going to spend it in Dallas at a swanky hotel."

"That sounds nice," Lola said.

Rider and Salina had found each other and were willing to wait to get married until Salina finished her schooling. Lola had never pictured Rider as a patient man, but he loved Salina with all of his heart and wanted her to follow her dreams. And she wanted to be a physicians assistant.

"Yeah, she needs the break. She's been studying really hard. I'm sure part of that break she'll be studying as well, but I'll take what I can get." He winked. "Are you ready to head to the house?"

Lola sighed. "I usually keep the shop open until five-thirty, but I guess my heart isn't into it today." She glanced around. "Let me shut things down and lock up, then I'll be ready to go."

"I'm off. I'm going to talk with the high school principal to see if I can use the gymnasium for my classes." She

PLAYING WITH FIRE

grinned. "I bet I can get some of the high school girls interested in learning some self-defense methods."

Lola snorted. "I was more interested in attracting the boys, not fighting them." She frowned. "You be careful out there. If Mateo wants to hurt people Daniel cares about, he might go after any one of the Graysons, including you."

Lily nodded. "I'll be vigilantly aware of my surroundings and not put myself at risk." The young woman left the shop and walked along Main Street in the direction of the high school.

"I swear she left for Paris a little girl and came back…" Rider shook his head.

"A badass woman with moves?" Lola suggested.

"Exactly. And all grown up." Rider smiled. "She's really come into her own."

"Yes, she has." Lola's chest swelled. "And she has a kind heart and loves children."

"You'd think after teaching kindergarten and spending summers with spoiled little rich kids, she'd have had enough." Rider chuckled. "Did she tell you about the time the little boy put a frog in her backpack?"

"No, but you can tell me while I work to close the shop." For the next fifteen minutes, Rider regaled Lola with stories Lily had related in letters home over the summer. By the time they exited the shoe shop, Lola was laughing and smiling. She loved all the members of the Grayson family. They were fixtures in the Hellfire community and had been for as long as she remembered.

By the time they reached her house, the sky had darkened, the clouds ending the day sooner than if the sun had been out and shining. Lola let herself into the house.

167

"If you don't mind, I'd like to look around," Rider said.

"Knock yourself out." Lola didn't want to admit she was glad he'd offered to chase out all the bogeymen. She followed him around. When he reached her bedroom, she opened the nightstand drawer and fished out her husband's prized handgun. "Just so you know, I have protection."

"Don't forget to put the magazine in the grip. It's not much use without bullets." He winked. "But you know that."

She twisted her lips. "I know that. I store it this way until I go to bed."

"As long as you're comfortable firing it, it's a good idea. Frankly, a can of wasp spray with a ten-foot range works as well to ward off unwanted visitors of the winged variety and two-legged kind."

She tilted her head. "I never thought of that."

"Hitting a guy in the eye with wasp spray gives you a chance to escape." He checked beneath the bed, in the closet and the adjoining bathroom. "Where's your attic?"

She led the way, remembering what had happened in the attic the last time she'd been up there. She wished Daniel was the one going through her house to make sure no one was hiding in it. But he was working a forty-eight-hour shift at the station. She suspected he'd called the Graysons for the favor of looking out for her.

When Rider was finished searching all the nooks and crannies, Lola smiled. "Thank you. I don't suppose you want to stay for a cup of coffee?"

Rider shook his head. "I need to get back to my shop. I have Raul Jemenez's truck up on the lift for an oil change and tire rotation. I promised I'd have it ready by morning."

Guilt flooded Lola. "I'm sorry. I'm keeping you from your business."

"Not at all. I needed the break. And I wanted to see what Lily was up to. I can't believe how good she is at the Krav Maga techniques. If I ever have little girls, their Aunt Lily better teach them what she knows."

"You'd make a wonderful father."

"I hope to, someday." He smiled. "I'll leave you to do your thing. If you need anything, don't hesitate to call. I can be here in a minute."

"Thanks, Rider." She hugged the man, her heart swelling with love and gratitude for what the Graysons were doing for her.

He let himself out the front door and waited to hear the lock click behind him before he walked the remainder of the way back to his shop.

Lola wandered into the living room and stared out the picture window at the murky dusk, a shiver rippling down the spine.

A movement across the street caught her attention. She thought she'd imagined it until it happened again. A shadow shifted at the corner of the big house with the wraparound porch on the opposite side of the street. Willa Dean Carmichael had converted her family home into a bed and breakfast. Sometimes guests stepped outside to smoke a cigarette.

When the shadow moved again, a figure detached itself from the corner, stepped out onto the sidewalk and stared across the road toward Lola's house.

She backed away from the window and dropped down on the couch. When she returned to the window, she eased up to the framework and peered outside.

The man had disappeared.

Lola should have been relieved, but a known menace was better than one she couldn't see.

She closed the blinds on the huge picture windows, went back to the front door and checked the deadbolt. Tomorrow, she'd consider putting in another deadbolt on both the front and the back doors. As soon as she could get someone out to her house, she'd have a security system installed. A woman couldn't be too careful when her life was at risk.

"WHY DON'T you take off work," Chance asked. "You're wearing a hole in the tile."

"I don't give a damn about the tile. And I can't leave. My backup is out of town until tomorrow morning when I come off duty."

"I can get one of the volunteers to stand in for you."

It was tempting, but Daniel wouldn't feel right if something happened that needed the expertise of a highly trained firefighter. The volunteers had training, but not all of them had experience. "One more night. I'll jog by Lola's later."

"Nash has the other deputies driving by at all hours. It's helpful that she lives on Main Street. They're even driving down the back alley, looking for anything suspicious."

Dan's cellphone buzzed in his pocket. He jumped and

dug it out. "Speaking of…" He hit the talk button and the speaker button. "Nash, tell me you have good news. Have you captured Mateo?"

"Sorry. We haven't. And it gets worse."

A heavy weight settled in the pit of Daniel's belly. "What now?"

"We found a body in a roadside ditch a couple miles south of town."

"Damn." Daniel muttered. "Male or female?"

"It's not Lola. I just spoke with Rider before the call came in. He made sure Lola got home safely and even did a walkthrough of her house. The man we found is Hispanic. He didn't have any documentation in his pockets, and I didn't recognize him."

"You think Mateo is at work scaring the people of the Hispanic community?"

"That would be my guess." Nash paused. "He was shot in the back of the head, Mateo's signature MO."

The lead weight sank deeper, making his gut twist and gurgle. "It's started," he whispered.

"It appears so. My contacts in the barrio are scared. They don't want to talk to me, and they're remaining indoors."

"That's not normal." The people of the barrio liked sitting outside. Some of their homes didn't have air-conditioning and were impossibly hot in the summertime. The men liked to sit outside in lawn chairs, drinking beer or tequila. The women gathered to gossip, letting the children run in the yards and streets.

"Yeah, it feels almost deserted and creepy." Nash said something to someone in the background. "Anyway, I thought I'd give you the heads-up. I have to get back to the investigation. We have the state crime lab out here, gathering evidence. I have to keep people from wandering in and mucking up the crime scene."

"Thanks, Nash. Be careful out there." Daniel ended the call and stared into Chance's eyes. "I might want to take the evening off after all. Who can we get to come in?"

"I'll get right on it." Chance pulled out his cellphone and browsed his contacts list. Before he could settle on one, the alarm went off in the fire station.

"What the hell?" Daniel punched the button on his handheld radio. "Flannigan here."

"Got a call that a house is on fire on the south side of Hellfire. And it appears to be spreading into the grass on the edge of town. I'll text the coordinates." The dispatcher sent the coordinates.

Already, Chance was suiting up in fire-retardant gear. "Where are we going?"

Daniel shook his head. "To the barrio."

Even before they had the truck out of the bay, three volunteer firefighters had arrived. Chance drove the pumper truck, while Daniel drove the ladder truck. The volunteers piled into one or the other.

As they sped south, they passed Lola's house.

Daniel shot a glance her way. The light glowed in the living room and upstairs bedroom. She was probably eating a solitary dinner. He wished he could be with her. But duty called. The houses on the south side of town were old tinderboxes, packed close together. They could burn in minutes, and hot, floating ash could ignite other structures nearby. The sooner they got there, the sooner they could stop the spread from one small house to another.

He handed his cellphone to the man in the seat beside him. "Look at my contacts. Find Lily and dial."

The man did as asked and hit the speaker button.

"Daniel?" Lily's voice sounded in the cab of the truck.

Without taking his gaze off the road, he said. "We think Mateo might make a move tonight. Could you go stay with Lola?"

"I can. But it'll take a few minutes. I just got out of the shower, and I'm at the ranch. But I'll be there as soon as I can."

"Thanks." Daniel ended the call and focused on getting the truck to the fire. As soon as they had the situation under control, he'd get one of the volunteers to ferry him back into Hellfire. Then he'd stay with Lola. If Mateo thought he could hurt her, he had another think coming.

CHAPTER 10

LOLA COULDN'T RELAX in her own home. What had once been a haven, was now a prison she had to endure to keep the bad guys out.

To keep busy, she went through the house, collecting the remainder of the photos of her and her husband, and started removing them from their frames. Eventually, she would scan them onto her computer and then place them in photo albums. She'd loved Engel with all her heart. Putting away his photos wasn't saying she didn't still love him. She would always love him.

Engel would want her to remember him, but he'd also said he wanted her to move on and find someone else to love. He knew she needed companionship.

After she gathered all the picture frames, she sat in the formal dining room she never used and continued to pull the photos out of their frames. One by one, she looked through them as she went, remembering each occasion and the fun they'd had along the way. He'd been a good man, and she was lucky they'd had so much time together.

A furry body rubbed against her ankle.

Lola leaned over to scratch her kitten's neck.

"Hey, Flannigan. Am I not giving you enough attention?" She lifted the kitten onto her lap and continued working. Flannigan curled into a ball and slept.

She was only halfway through the stack of frames when she heard a loud crash, like shattering glass.

Her heart skipped several beats, and she froze for a moment. Then she jumped up from her chair, looking frantically for her cellphone. Her heart sank when she remembered she'd left it in the kitchen on the counter. The same direction the sound of shattered glass had come from.

More glass breakage sounded, followed by the click of the door lock being opened.

She wouldn't have time to run through the living room to the front door, and the back door had been compromised. With her heart lodged in her throat, Lola ran for the staircase, her bare feet making no noise on the wooden floor. She took the steps two at a time and darted down the hallway, praying they hadn't seen her headed that way. Once inside the master bedroom, she quietly closed the door and ran to the nightstand where she'd left the gun.

Footsteps pounded up the staircase.

She fumbled with the handgun, slid the magazine into the handle and locked it in place.

The lock on the bedroom door wouldn't be hard to break. One good kick and…

The door crashed open, hitting the wall on the other side.

A man with dark hair, black eyes and tattoos everywhere she could see stepped through the door.

She aimed the gun at his chest. "Stop, or I'll shoot," she said in her best commanding voice.

"Shoot," Mateo said as he stalked toward her.

Her hand shaking, Lola squeezed the trigger.

Nothing happened.

She'd forgotten to chamber a round like Engel had taught her all those years ago. Lola grabbed the top of the gun, but before she could pull it back, Mateo was on her. She hit him in the side of the head with the gun, but not with enough force to knock him out.

He grunted and grabbed her wrists, shaking them hard. The handgun dropped from her fingers.

Lola's heart dropped into the pit of her belly. She didn't have a weapon to fight this man.

Then she remembered one of the other moves Lily had showed her. She jerked up her knee and hit him in the balls.

The man cursed and bent over. She raised her knee again and hit him in the nose.

His hands loosened their grip on her wrists, and she yanked them free. Grabbing his shirt, she pulled him forward, ducked out of the way, and he slammed against the wall. Then she ran for the bedroom door.

A large Hispanic man stepped through the doorframe.

Moving too fast to slow down at the last second, she plowed into him. He grabbed her around the middle, trapping her arms against her sides. Too close to get leverage, she couldn't knee him in the groin. Without her hands, she couldn't poke him in the eyes. She hadn't gotten to the lesson that would get her out of this hold.

A hand grabbed a chunk of her hair and yanked hard.

Her eyes watering, Lola refused to cry. These men were monsters. They would show no pity. And they'd never let her go, willingly. If she wanted out of this situation, she'd have to figure it out herself.

The gun she'd hoped to kill him with was now pointed at her temple.

"I heard Flannigan had another bitch," he said, his face so close to hers, she could smell his bad breath.

Her stomach roiled. "I don't know what you're talking about."

"You're Flannigan's new bitch. My brother killed the other. And he killed my brother."

"Again," she said. "I don't know what you're talking about. Who's Flannigan?"

He yanked her hair harder. "You lie. I saw him here last night, panting after you like the dog he is." He nodded toward the man holding her and said something in Spanish.

Lola wished she'd taken Spanish seriously when she'd been in high school.

The man tightened his hold and half-dragged, half-carried her out of the room.

Refusing to make it any easier on the guy, Lola went limp.

Instead of heading downstairs and out of the house, he started up the stairs to the attic.

That didn't make any sense to Lola. If they wanted to kidnap her to lure Daniel out into the open, putting her in the attic made it all too easy for the authorities to surround them.

As the big man climbed the stairs, Lola waited until he was halfway up, then she stiffened, planted her feet on the next step and pushed backward with all her might. The man teetered and fell hard on his back, sliding down the steps, still holding onto her, though his grip slipped.

As soon as she could get her feet beneath her, she scrambled up, stepped over the man and ran straight into Mateo. He backhanded her so hard, she slammed against the wall. Stars swam in her vision. Too stunned to do anything, Lola couldn't see straight to fight back.

Mateo grabbed her from behind, again pinning her arms to her sides. The other man gripped her ankles in iron paws. Together, they carried her up the steps into the attic and sat her on an old wooden straight back chair. While Mateo continued to hold onto her, the other man found a roll of duct tape and secured her ankles to the chair. Then he wrapped the tape around her body, trapping her arms against her sides.

Thankfully, they didn't apply the tape over her mouth. Instead, Mateo laid her cellphone on the floor beside her.

"Flannigan will suffer as I have suffered when I lost someone I loved. And he will have to listen to your screams as you die."

Fear stole Lola's breath away. The look of pure evil in Mateo's eyes terrified her. Was he going to torture her until she screamed for mercy?

He spoke in rapid Spanish to the other man. The only word she recognized was *gasolina*. Gasoline. What would they do with...? Her heart froze in her chest. They were going to burn her house down...with her in it.

Mateo touched her phone's screen and went through her contacts until he found Daniel's number. He pressed it and put the phone on speaker.

After four rings, Daniel answered. "Lola? Are you okay?"

For a moment, Lola didn't say anything. She didn't know what to say or do. If Daniel came to save her, Mateo would be there to kill him.

When she didn't speak, Mateo did. "I have your woman."

The line went silent but for shouts in the background.

"You hurt her at all, I swear I'll find you and rip you apart, piece by piece."

Mateo snorted. "You will suffer as I did when you murdered my brother."

"He killed my partner," Daniel said. "Lola hasn't done anything to you. Nothing. Leave her out of this."

"Too late." Mateo's lip curled in a sneer. "Now, listen to her screams."

"Son of a bitch," Daniel said. "I'll kill you, Mateo!"

Mateo left the attic, closing the door behind him. She heard the key twist in the lock, and then the snap of metal.

Holy shit. He'd broken off a key in the lock. Even if she could free herself from the duct tape, she would have to break down the door to get out.

"Lola," Daniel called out. "Hang on, I'm coming."

"No," she said. "He'll be waiting. He'll kill you."

"I don't care. I won't want to live if you die." He

shouted to someone, "Mateo has Lola, he's going to kill her. I'm taking your truck."

"I'm coming with you," said a voice in the background that sounded like Becket. "I'll let Nash know."

"And call the state troopers, ICE, the national guard," Daniel said. "Anyone you can think of. We have to get to her in time, and Mateo has to die."

Though her life should be flashing before her, Lola chuckled. "Isn't that overkill? Pun intended. And by the way, he's going to burn down my house. Please do what you can to save the others around me."

For a moment, Daniel was silent. "He's going to burn your house down? Lola, where are you?"

She didn't want to answer. Going into a burning house was bad enough, but going up into the attic would be deadly.

"Lola, honey, answer me," Daniel begged.

"I'm in the attic."

DANIEL DROVE BECKET'S TRUCK, breaking every speed limit between the fire south of town to Hellfire. Becket sat beside him, his fingers in a death-grip around the oh-shit handle above his door.

"Keep talking to me, Lola," Daniel said.

"What do you want me to say?" She grunted and a tapping sound echoed through the phone.

"What are you doing?" he asked.

"Trying to break this chair they taped me to."

Another loud bang was accompanied by the sound of splitting wood and another grunt.

"Lola?"

"I'm okay," she said, a little breathless. "Just broke the legs on the chair and did a face plant against the old sofa. You remember the one."

Daniel smiled, though his heart was breaking into a million pieces.

"Damn. I smell smoke," she said. "Got...to...get out...of this...damned tape."

"Find a beam or something jagged to rub the tape against. Wasn't there a beam in the middle of the attic?" Daniel tried to remember what he'd seen in Lola's attic. But all he could remember was making love to her on that old sofa.

"Making my way over to it." She coughed. "The smoke is getting thicker."

Beside him Becket's phone rang. He glanced down at the caller ID. "It's Lily." He pressed the talk button and speaker. "Lily, where are you?"

"I'm on Main Street. Lola's house is on fire."

"Be careful. Mateo is around, and we don't know who else is with him."

"Where's Lola?" Lily asked.

"In her house."

"God damn the bastard!" Lily exclaimed. "I'm going in."

"No," Lola said. "Don't let her get close to the house. Mateo might shoot anyone who tries to get to me or put out the fire."

"Is that Lola?" Lily asked.

"She's on Daniel's phone."

"Can she get out of the house?" Lily asked.

"Not yet," Lola said. "But I'm trying."

"Sweet Jesus," Lily said. "I see a sheriff's car pulling up. If we can get past Mateo, we're going in."

"Don't," Lola said.

But Lily ended the call.

"That girl is entirely too headstrong," Becket bit out.

"It'll carry her a long way through life. Please," Lola said. "If I don't make it out of here, tell her I love her like the daughter I never had. She's amazing."

"You're going to make it," Daniel said. "I owe you a date. I won't be able to live with myself if I can't make it up to you."

"Thank you, Daniel," Lola said. "If you hadn't been the one to come get me off the roof, I might never have decided to move on and live in the present with hope for the future. I guess it's fitting my old photos go up in flames. I didn't have anyone to leave them to. Since my husband and I didn't have children, there's no one left to mourn my demise. At least there's that." She grunted.

"You're not giving up, are you?" Daniel asked. "Because I'm not giving up on you. Your whole life is ahead of you. And I plan on being a part of it."

"What if I don't want you to?"

Her words stabbed him in the heart, but deep down, he knew she didn't mean them. She couldn't, not after the way she'd kissed him last night. "You'd be lying."

"You're right. Somewhere between your trying to teach me a lesson and me trying to show you how it's done, I fell in love with you." Lola coughed.

"Hang in there, Lola," Becket said. "We're almost to Hellfire."

"Please, don't come," she coughed again. "It's too late to save me, and Mateo is waiting for you. He'll kill you."

"Not if I kill him first," Daniel said, his fingers clutching the steering wheel so tightly his knuckles turned white. "We're coming."

"Please...don't," she said and burst into a fit of coughing.

"Lola, honey, we'll get you out of there," Daniel promised, though he didn't yet know how. "I'm coming for you. I won't let you die, because I love you."

"You don't believe in..." she paused to cough, "commitment."

"You made me see the light. I didn't believe in commitment until I met you." He drove into Hellfire, not slowing until he neared Lola's house on Main Street. Flames licked the sky, reflecting off the low-slung cloud cover. If only it would rain. "Please rain," Daniel muttered.

The firetrucks might not make it back to town in time to douse the inferno. They needed a miracle.

Then a man stepped out into the street and raised his arms, holding something in his hands.

"Duck!" Becket yelled.

Daniel ducked just before a bullet ripped through the windshield and buried itself in the headrest behind him. "It's Mateo."

Becket pulled his handgun from the glove box and tapped the magazine into the handle. "If you get me close enough, I'll shoot the bastard."

"I have a better idea, but it requires you to stay low." He slammed his foot to the floor and headed straight for the man in the street.

Mateo unloaded his magazine into the oncoming truck. At the last minute, he dove to the right.

Daniel anticipated his move and swerved to the right, hitting Mateo. His body launched into the air and landed several feet away.

"Look out!" Becket yelled.

Daniel ducked. Another barrage of bullets rained in at them from the driver's side.

"Give me the gun," Daniel demanded.

Becket handed over the pistol, keeping low as the bullets continued to fly.

In a gap between rounds, Daniel dared to lift his head high enough he could see the man shooting at them. "I'm getting out," he said.

"He'll shoot you."

"I have to take the chance. We can't waste any more time." The glow of her house burning illuminated the interior of the truck. For all Daniel knew, he might already be too late.

Another round of bullets pelted the side of the truck.

Daniel pushed open the door, dropped to the ground and rolled beneath the chassis. Bullets glinted off the pavement but missed him. He found his target, lined up his sights and pulled the trigger. One bullet was all he needed. The man swayed then fell face-first to the ground.

Daniel rolled out from under the truck and ran for the house.

When he tried the door, it wouldn't open.

He tried kicking it in, but the deadbolt held strong.

Behind him the truck engine revved. "Get out of the way," Becket yelled.

Daniel stood back.

Becket drove the truck straight for the front door, hitting it hard enough to cave the wall in and knock the door flat. Then he backed up and jumped down.

Daniel didn't wait for him. He pulled his shirt up over his mouth and nose and ran into the burning house.

CHAPTER 11

FROM WHAT HE COULD TELL, Mateo had used gasoline as an accelerant, sloshing it over the interior of the house. Flames had consumed the curtains and were eating into the walls and furnishings. Some flames had started up the side of the staircase.

Daniel didn't care that the heat inside the house felt like a broiler oven. Lola was in the attic. He had to get there.

Up the stairs, taking two at time, he ran as fast as he could. On the second floor, the smoke was thicker and the rooms were on fire. Daniel could smell the gasoline they must have doused the beds with. He passed the bedrooms on either side of the hallway and climbed the stairs to the attic, his eyes burning and his lungs on fire. The attic door was closed. He turned the handle and pushed, but the door wouldn't open, and time was running out for Lola and for him. He'd succumb to smoke inhalation soon if he didn't get her out.

Turning to his side, he slammed his shoulder into the door. It didn't budge.

He wouldn't give up. Lola needed him. He couldn't let her die. It was all his fault she was targeted in the first place. He refused to hold her lifeless body in his arms. She had to live.

He hit the door again with every ounce of his weight and strength.

The sound of wood splintering gave him hope.

When he hit the door again, it burst open, and he fell inside, landing on the floor beside Lola's still form, still wrapped in duct tape, half a chair keeping her in the sitting position.

"Lola, honey," he said, his voice coming out like a croak. "Please be alive." He climbed to his feet, his head in the smoke now. He bent and lifted Lola's body into his arms and started for the door.

Smoke billowed up the stairs into the room, blinding him. He squeezed shut his eyes and then opened them, determined to get the hell out of the house, with his woman in his arms.

Once he made it past the top of the attic stairs and started down, the smoke wasn't quite as bad. Unfortunately, the flames had consumed the staircase to the ground floor and were eating into the walls.

Searching for another way out, he pushed into a room Mateo had missed with the gasoline. It appeared to be a small bedroom that had been converted into a shoe closet. On the far end was a window just large enough to fit a person through it.

He hurried forward, laid Lola on the floor and tried to

open the window. Several coats of paint over the years had sealed the window shut. The room had a desk and a wooden straight back chair. Daniel grabbed the chair and swung it at the window. Glass shattered. He cleared the shards away from the window and peered out. The window opened out onto the porch roof. If the fire didn't get to the porch for a few minutes, he might have a shot at getting Lola out of the house and to safety.

He lifted Lola in his arms and pushed her through the window, easing her down onto the porch roof, his arms straining to keep her from rolling over the edge.

He climbed out behind her and waved to the people gathered around the burning house. "Bring a ladder. I have Lola."

Becket ran to his truck where he kept a spare ladder for checking the level of corn in his grain bins.

The fire had consumed much of the interior of the house and was working its way outward.

Lola rolled over and blinked her eyes open. "Flannigan," she croaked.

"I'm here, sweetie."

"No," she coughed. "My kitten, Flannigan."

"The cat's still in there?" He glanced back at the inferno that had been her house.

"Flannigan," she said, her voice barely a croak. "Must save. He doesn't deserved to die."

"Neither do you. But I'm not leaving you until you're safely on the ground."

She tried to rise up, but her arms were still taped to the chair back. "She likes to hide out in my shoe closet." Lola burst into a coughing fit. "Let me find her."

Daniel shook his head. "You're not going anywhere but to the ground."

"But she'll die," Lola's eyes filled, and tears spilled down her face.

Sirens sounded in the distance, moving closer. A ladder appeared over the edge of the roof, and Becket climbed up. "Thank God, you found her."

"Take her," Daniel said. "I'm going back in for the cat."

"Are you crazy?" Becket stared at him as if he'd lost his mind. "The floors and ceilings are about to collapse."

"I can't let my namesake die." He dove back into the window, praying the cat lived up to its owner's claim and liked hiding out in her shoe closet. If the cat had hidden anywhere else in the house, it hadn't survived.

With limited lighting and thickening smoke, Daniel felt his way along until he encountered something other than shoes. When his hand touched something furry, he grabbed hold of it and pulled it out from behind an array of skinny stiletto heels. The cat was limp and barely breathing, but if Daniel could get it outside into fresh, smoke-free air, it might have a chance.

Keeping his head as low as possible, he cradled the kitten in his arms and crawled through the window out onto the porch roof.

Becket had just reached the ground with Lola—chair, tape and all—slung over his shoulder in a fireman's carry. Others helped him carry her far enough away from the blaze before they laid her on the ground.

The fire trucks arrived and an ambulance.

Daniel climbed down the ladder and carried the kitten to Lola. "I found her," he said.

Emergency Medical Technicians were cutting away at the tape binding Lola to the chair. They'd fitted an oxygen mask over her face and were taking her vitals. Beneath the mask, her lips curved into a smile. "Thank you," she said, her voice little more than a croak. Then she burst into a fit of coughing.

Daniel turned to the EMTs. "You got a mask small enough for this little thing?"

The EMT grinned. "Actually, we do." He unearthed a small mask attached to an oxygen bottle. "We keep one just for the pets found in a fire." He showed Daniel how to use it and handed it over.

"We need to check you out, as well," the paramedic said.

"I'm okay," Daniel said and proceeded to cough up a lung. At least, it felt like he did.

The EMT shook his head and handed Daniel an oxygen mask. "You're a firefighter, you know smoke inhalation can be tricky. Don't argue, just wear the mask and enjoy the free ride to the hospital."

"As long as I go with her." Daniel tipped his chin toward Lola. "And the cat comes, too."

The paramedic frowned. "You can ride with her, but we can't transport animals."

"She's an emotional support animal. If she doesn't come, Ms. Engel will be emotionally distraught, even more so than she is now."

"Do you have documents proving the animal is an emotional support animal?" the EMT asked.

"I'm sure she did, but it's somewhere in that burning building," Daniel lied. "Come on…" He leaned close and read the man's name tag. "Mr. Williams, have a heart. They almost died tonight."

The medical technician's frown deepened. "As long as you don't tell a soul."

Daniel nodded, fitting the mask over his mouth. "My lips are sealed."

As they loaded Lola into the ambulance, Daniel met with Nash, Rider, Becket and Chance, who'd arrived while he'd been inside Lola's house. He pulled off his oxygen mask. "Did we get Mateo?"

"We did," Nash said. "They're taking him to the county hospital."

"They need to make sure he has guards on him all the time," Daniel said, regretting that he hadn't killed the man when he'd hit him with the truck.

"He's not going anywhere anytime soon. He has two broken legs and a broken hip. The man is in severe pain, and the EMTs aren't inclined to give him any pain meds." Nash smiled. "And we got the other guy. He died of a gunshot wound."

At least he'd gotten one of them. "I wish I'd hit Mateo even harder. He doesn't deserve to live after what he tried to do to Lola. He needs to be off the street permanently… six feet under."

"Oh, I think he'll be off the street at the very least."

Daniel snorted. "Until the feds decide they want to trade him again."

"I don't think that'll happen. Not after all the trouble he caused in Hellfire." Nash jerked his head toward several news reporters standing behind the sheriff's yellow tape. "As you can see, the news teams are covering the incident, and Lily's right in the middle of it, making sure they know who was responsible."

"Given his reputation, they should never have let him go to begin with. What the hell good does it do for the border patrol to do their job, only to have politicians screw it up?"

"And that's why you're working for the Hellfire Fire Department." Chance pounded Daniel on the back, sending him into a fit of coughing. The kitten in his arms moved, sinking her little claws into his skin. "Ouch! Hey, I'm on your side."

"Dude, you should have that cough checked out," Chance said.

"I'm going to the hospital." Daniel said.

Chance pointed at the ball of smoky fur in Daniel's hand. "I didn't know you were a cat person."

"I'm not," Daniel said. "The kitten belongs to Lola." And if it meant everything to her, he'd take care of it until she was able to care for it herself.

The ambulance driver waved to him.

"That's my cue. If you need me, I'll be at the hospital with Lola."

"We'll stop by after we clean up this mess," Becket assured him. "I know Lily will want to see Lola. Same with Kinsey and Phoebe."

"Give her until morning. Hopefully, she'll be out of the woods by then." Daniel slid the oxygen mask over his nose and mouth, climbed into the back of the ambulance and sat next to the paramedic working with Lola.

He'd started an IV and was monitoring her breathing.

Lola raised the arm with the IV, her head turning toward Daniel.

He clasped her hand, careful not to disturb the IV. "I'm here, sweetheart," he said, his voice muffled by the plastic mask.

"Mateo?" she whispered.

Daniel could barely hear her through the oxygen mask covering her mouth and nose. He pulled his off so that she could hear him better. "On his way to the hospital with two broken legs and possible internal injuries."

She closed her eyes. "Thank God. The other man?"

"Dead."

She nodded and lay still, her hand limp inside his. For a moment, he thought she'd passed out. But then she squeezed his fingers ever so slightly. "Thank you for saving Flannigan."

The kitten had snuggled in the curve of his arm, no longer in need of the oxygen bottle.

"I think she likes me."

"It's a he," Lola said.

"Nope. I know my animal parts. This is a girl kitten."

"I guess I can't call her Flannigan."

He chuckled. "You can call her anything you want."

"Lucky."

"Yes, you are. You're lucky to be alive. Had you been inside that attic any longer, I don't know what would have happened." He knew, and it still made his gut knot. The fire would have eaten into the flooring and the attic would have crashed down onto the floor below to be consumed in flames. Lola wouldn't have known because she'd have died of smoke inhalation before that happened.

"Glad you're safe," she said and coughed.

"I'm glad you are, too." He brought her hand to his lips. "Now, stop talking. I know it hurts." His lungs and throat hurt, but he hadn't been exposed to the smoke nearly as long as Lola. He fitted his mask over his face and breathed in the oxygen.

The rest of the trip passed in silence. When they arrived at the hospital, Daniel tucked the kitten into his firefighting jacket and zipped it. He and Lola were ushered into separate examination rooms.

"I'm fine. I'd rather stay with Ms. Engel."

"You're a firefighter," the nurse said. "You know how dangerous smoke inhalation can be. Let the doctor check you over, then you can look in on Ms. Engel."

"Have him look at her first. I can wait." The kitten wiggled beneath his jacket.

"Could you remove your jacket so that I can get your vital signs?"

Daniel turned his back to the woman and shrugged out of the jacket.

The kitten clung to his shirt during the process.

Once he had the jacket off, he tucked the kitten into the folds and laid it on a chair on the opposite side of the gurney from the nurse. Then he sat on the edge of the gurney, getting soot on the white sheets.

The kitten seemed content to curl up in his warm jacket for the moment.

After she took his blood pressure, temperature and pulse, the nurse left the room.

Daniel strained to hear what was going on in the next room, but he couldn't discern any words. However, since there was no code blue, he assumed Lola was still breathing.

Finally, the doctor rounded the corner from Lola's room and moved into Daniel's. "I hear there was some excitement in Hellfire," the doctor said.

"Yes, sir." Daniel was past patient and ready to charge out the door.

"Relax," the doctor said. "Ms. Engel is going to be all right. We'll keep her overnight for observation, but she should be able to go home tomorrow."

"She can't. Her house burned to the ground."

"Oh." The doctor stopped before placing his stethoscope on Daniel's chest. "I'm sorry to hear that. I can have one of the nurses contact the Red Cross. They can provide temporary lodging and a variety of sundries for people in Ms. Engel's situation."

"We'll take care of her," Daniel said gruffly.

The doctor performed his exam and announced, "You have mild smoke inhalation, but I don't think it presents a risk to you. I'll sign your discharge papers, and we can have you out of here in the next twenty minutes."

Daniel shook his head. "I'm not leaving until Lola… Ms. Engel leaves."

The doctor nodded. "She'll be moved to a regular room where she can be monitored overnight. As soon as we get a room assignment, I'll have the nurses let you know where she is." The doctor smiled. "And keep the kitten under wraps. They frown on animals in the sterile environments."

"She was in the fire, too. And she means a lot to Ms. Engel."

"I understand. Don't worry, I didn't see a thing." He winked and left the room.

Minutes later, he was discharged, but he moved from his room over to Lola's. When they wheeled her out of the ER, he was with her all the way, holding the kitten beneath his jacket in one hand, his other hand clasped firmly around Lola's.

Once they arrived in the room, he stepped back to allow the nurses to do their job and get the patient transferred to the bed. Once they had her settled and all the monitoring equipment reestablished, they disappeared, leaving Lola alone with Daniel and Flannigan the female kitten.

He pulled a chair up to her bed and laid the kitten close to her hand.

"She's covered in soot," Lola said in a hoarse whisper.

Daniel chuckled. "None of us have had a chance to clean up."

Lola closed her eyes and lay still for a long time. "My house?" she finally asked.

Daniel didn't want to tell her it was a complete loss. Sometimes news like that made it even harder for a patient to recuperate.

"I take it by your silence that it's a total loss." She opened one eye, stared at him and then closed the eye. "My husband and I made a lot of good memories in that house."

Daniel had to lean close to hear her whispered words. "I'm sorry, Lola."

She twisted her lips wryly. "I guess it means I have to

make a clean start. The memories are still with me. It's just the things that are gone."

"And I'm sorry about your shoe closet. I know it meant a lot to you."

She laughed and coughed. "I own a shoe store. I know where to get new shoes. The question is, where will I live until I figure out what to do? Should I buy a house or rebuild the one I had?" She pinched the bridge of her nose.

"I think the decision can wait until you feel better. And if you need a place to stay…I have room in the cabin I'm renting from the Graysons."

She opened her eyes and frowned. "You'd do that? Mr. I'm-not-into-commitment?" She shook her head. "Why the change of heart?"

"I met a woman," he said. "We did a thing." His tone lowered as he voiced what had been growing inside him since he and Lola started their affair. "I fell in love."

She closed her eyes and lay back against the pillow, her face smudged with soot, still beautiful despite the circumstances. "Why would you fall in love with me? I'm ten years older than you. You could have any woman in Texas. Why me?"

"Because you're fun, spunky and you care about people."

"I care about you," she said so softly he barely heard her.

"Age is only a number. It's what is in the heart that matters," Daniel said.

A smile pulled up the corners of her lips. "I never expected Daniel Flannigan to wax poetic with anyone.

But that was beautiful." She reached for his hand and brought it to her lips where she pressed a kiss to the back of his knuckles. "I never thought I'd find someone I could love as much as I loved Engel." She paused. "And I didn't."

Daniel's chest tightened. She was going to let him down, call it off, tell him she didn't love him. God, he'd jumped the gun and spoken too soon.

"I don't love you like I loved Engel. I love you differently. Because you're a different person than he was." She broke into a coughing fit.

Daniel's heart swelled as he handed her the cup of ice water the nurse had left for her.

Lola sipped and lay back against the pillow. "I love that you're good at proving a point. That you care about the people around you and that you take lovemaking to a whole different level. I'd never had sex against the wall before I met you." She smiled. "And you're willing to experiment. You're fierce and passionate about everything you do, for the fire department, for me and for your friends."

"So? What are we going to do about this thing between us?" Daniel asked.

EPILOGUE

Two weeks later.

"Daniel, can you bring that tray of steaks out with you?" Lola leaned into the back door of the Grayson ranch house. "The chicken breasts are almost done."

"I can take over now," Becket said. "The animals are all fed, and I've had my shower, so I don't smell like any of them." He winked and took the spatula from her hand.

"I don't mind cooking. Not that I do it that often. Daniel is much better at it than I am."

Daniel backed out the door, carrying a large platter of raw steak. "I had to learn to cook out of self-preservation. The guys at the fire station tried to kill me with chicken nuggets and tater tots. A man cannot survive on chicken nuggets and tater tots."

"Speak for yourself." Chance patted his flat stomach. "They beat MREs any day."

Nash stepped out on the porch with Phoebe on his

arm. "What? You don't like MREs? I thought all army guys liked MREs."

"Yeah. Right." Chance shook his head. "If I never have to eat one of those again, it's fine by me."

Lola turned to Nash. "I hear the sheriff's department hired a new deputy."

Nash's brow dipped. "We did. I'm not sure what to think about her yet."

Lola's brows rose. "Her?"

He nodded. "She's prior army military police corps."

Daniel glanced over at Chance, sitting on the porch steps. "She and Chance ought to have some stories to share. What are the chances they know each other?"

"One in three or four hundred thousand," Chance said. "What's her name?"

"Kate Bradley," Nash replied. "She starts next week. She's having a hard time finding a place to live."

"My garage apartment survived the fire," Lola said. "If she doesn't mind the smell of smoke next door."

"I'll let her know. Only one problem you might not agree to," Nash paused. "She has a seventy-five-pound Belgian Malinois, a retired military war dog, that'll be living with her."

Lola smiled. "I love dogs. As long as she cleans up after it, she's welcome to stay in the garage apartment."

"Have you decided what you're going to do about your house?" Kinsey asked from where she sat on the porch swing.

"Insurance will cover the cost of rebuilding. I'm just not sure *where* I want to rebuild." She shot a smile toward

PLAYING WITH FIRE

Daniel. "Or should I say I'm not sure where *we* want to build."

Lily came off the porch railing where she'd been perched. "Wait…what?"

"You heard her," Daniel said with his back to the crowd. He laid the last steak on the grill and let Becket take over. The he turned with a serious look on his face. "We're not sure where we want to build. Are you going to show them?"

Lola smiled so widely she thought her face might split in half. Then she held her left hand up, displaying a shiny new diamond ring. "Daniel asked. I said yes, and…we're getting married!"

"No way!" Lily said and was the first to hug Lola, squeezing her so tightly, she couldn't breathe. "I'm so happy for you."

Phoebe and Kinsey were next, both hugging her and then admiring her ring.

"That was fast," Kinsey said. "What made you decide this was what you two wanted?"

Lola laughed. "Well, let's see, he got me down off my rooftop, ran over the bad guy, saved me from a fire and rescued my kitten. He wasn't able to save my shoe collection, but I cut him some slack." She winked at Daniel. "After all that trouble, I kinda felt sorry for him and agreed to be his wife. You know…a pity yes."

Daniel shook his head and walked up the steps to stand in front of her on the porch. "It was something like that. But not quite." He pulled her into his arms. "I like a determined woman. Lola worked hard to get the attention of another man..." He shot a glare at Chance. "Several times, she called the fire department for some trumped-up emergency. I just happened to respond to the calls and wanted to teach her a lesson regarding what constitutes an emergency." He kissed the top of her head. "But she ended up teaching me a thing or two that I can't go into because it's not nice to kiss and tell. And then she tells me not to try to save her because it would be too dangerous. Well, we all know I joined the Hellfire Fire Department because I thrive on danger, being the big bad hero that I am, so I pulled her out of the fire. And as the hero, she became all starry-eyed and begged me to marry her."

Lola laughed, her eyes dancing. "Okay, so maybe I did say I wouldn't be opposed to building a house together. But I didn't ask you to marry me, and I certainly didn't beg. I have my pride, after all."

Lily laughed. "Somewhere between Daniel's story and Lola's has to be the truth." She hugged Daniel. "I don't care. I'm just happy to see you two so happy. You deserve it."

"And to think," Chance said as he hugged Lola. "That could have been me rescuing you, and this story would have had a very different ending." He shook Daniel's hand. "Don't screw it up. I'm watching you."

"There's someone out there for you," Lily said. "She just hasn't shown up yet. Maybe our new sheriff's deputy will be the one." She gave her brother a sly look. "You like dogs, don't you?"

"I like dogs, but I don't need a matchmaker setting me up with the new girl in town. I can find my own woman when I'm ready to settle down." He gave Lily a hard glare. "And I'm not ready to settle down."

"You say that but look at you. You've been back from your army commitment for a couple years, and you've yet to settle down." Lily planted a hand on her hip. "You need a partner in life to come home to. Someone who can calm your crazy ass down."

He held up his hand. "Stop right there. I don't need my punk kid sister telling me how to live my life."

Daniel steered Lola away from the argument and out to the corral fence then turned her to face him.

Lola looked up into the eyes of the man she loved so much. "Is there something you wanted to say that you didn't want the others to hear?"

"Yes." Daniel kissed the tip of her nose. "I wanted to tell you that I don't expect you to forget your life with your husband. It's a part of you and what makes you so special. I also wanted to let you know how happy you make me. I won't try to be someone I'm not, but I promise to be the best me you deserve."

Lola wrapped her arms around his neck and leaned up on her toes to kiss him. "And I promise to love you with all of my heart. I'm not your Casey, and I'm not a badass border agent, but I will be the best person I can be for you. But one thing…you have to promise to build me a shoe closet in our new house."

"You got it." He wrapped his arms around her waist and bent to kiss her long and hard. "I can't believe I finally found you."

"You found me?" She laughed. "I thought I found you."

"I think Flannigan brought us together," Daniel said.

"I'm going to feed that cat tuna for the rest of her life. She's the best matchmaker a woman could ever hope for." Lola cupped the back of Daniel's neck. "Now, kiss me like you mean it. We have an audience, I'm wearing a diamond ring and my brand new Christian Louboutins and I'm all for giving them a good show."

Daniel bent her over his arm, sweeping her low to the ground and kissed her like the Hollywood heroes did in the movies. But it was even better because he was her hero, and he would be hers until death do they part.

VOODOO ON THE BAYOU

CAJUN MAGIC MYSTERY SERIES #1

New York Times & *USA Today*
Bestselling Author

ELLE JAMES

Don't piss off the Voodoo Queen ...

VOODOO
ON THE
BAYOU

A CAJUN MAGIC MYSTERY

ELLE JAMES

CHAPTER 1

Bayou Miste, deep in the Atchafalaya Basin of southern Louisiana
June

Bound to a cypress tree, Craig Thibodeaux struggled to free his hands, the coarse rope rubbing his wrists raw with the effort. A fat bayou mosquito buzzed past his ear to feast on his unprotected skin. The bulging insect had plenty of blood in its belly—much more and the flying menace would be grounded.

What I wouldn't give for a can of bug repellent.

Craig shook his head violently in hopes of discouraging the little scavenger from landing.

The dark-skinned Cajuns who'd kidnapped him stood guard on either side of him, their legs planted wide and arms crossed over bare muscular chests. They looked like rejected cast members from a low-budget barbarian movie, and they didn't appear affected in the least by the blood-sucking mosquitoes.

"Hey, Mo, don't you think you guys are taking this a little too far?" Craig aimed a sharp blast of breath at a bug crawling along his shoulder. "I swear I won that card game fair and square."

The man on his right didn't turn his way or flick an eyelid.

Craig looked to his left. "Come on Larry, we've been friends since you and I got caught snitching apples from Old Lady Reneau's orchard. Let me go."

Larry didn't twitch a muscle, as if Craig hadn't uttered a word.

"If it will make you feel any better, I'll give you back your money," Craig offered, although he'd really won that game.

He'd known Maurice Saulnier and Lawrence Ezell since he was a snot-nosed kid spending his summer vacations with his Uncle Joe in the southern Louisiana town of Bayou Miste. He had considered them friends. Until now.

Granted, Craig had been back for less than a week after an eight-year sojourn into the legal jungles of the New Orleans court system. But his absence shouldn't be a reason for them to act the way they were. An odd sensation tickled his senses, as if foreshadowing something unpleasant waiting to happen. Sweat dripped off his brow, the heat and humidity of the swamp oppressive.

"Look guys, whatever you're planning, you won't get away with it." Craig strained against the bonds holding him tight to the rough bark of the cypress tree.

"Ah, *mon cher*, but we will." A low, musical voice reached out of the darkness preceding the appearance of a woman. She wore a flowing, bright red caftan with a sash tied around her ample girth and a matching kerchief covering her hair. Although large, she floated into the firelight, her bone necklace rattling in time to a steady drumbeat building in the shadows. Her skin was a light brown, almost mocha, weathered by the elements and age. Her dark brown eyes shone brightly, the flames of a nearby fire dancing in their depths.

Despite the weighty warmth of the swamp, a chill crept down Craig's spine. "Who's the lady in the muumuu?"

The silent wonder next to him deigned to speak in a reverent whisper, "Madame LeBieu."

Craig frowned and mentally scratched his head. Madame LeBieu...Madame LeBieu...oh, yes. The infamous Bayou Miste Voodoo priestess, a notorious mishmash of Cajun-Caribbean witchdoctor mumbo-jumbo and healer. No one really knew her background, but she was both feared and revered in the community. He studied her with more interest and a touch of unease. Was he to be a sacrifice in some wacky Voodoo ceremony?

"Are you in charge of these two thugs?" Craig feigned a cockiness he didn't feel.

"It be I who called upon dem." She dipped her head in a regal nod.

"Then call them off and untie me." Craig shot an angry look at the men on either side of him. "You've obviously got the wrong guy."

"Were you not de man what be goin' out with de sweet Lisa LeBieu earlier dis very evening?"

"Yes," Craig said, caution stretching his answer, as dread pooled in his stomach. He didn't go into the fact that Lisa wasn't so sweet. "Why?"

"I be Madame LeBieu and Lisa be *ma petite fille*. She say you dally with her heart and cast it aside." The woman's rich, melodious voice held a thread of steel.

Craig frowned in confusion. "You mean this isn't about the card game? This is about Lisa, your granddaughter?"

"No, dis be 'bout you mistreatment of *les femmes*."

"I don't get it. I didn't touch her. She came on to me, and I took her home."

"Abuse not always takes de physical form. You shunned her love and damage her chakras. For dis, you pay."

Craig cocked an eyebrow in disbelief. "You mean I was conked on the head and dragged from my bed all because I refused to sleep with your granddaughter?" He snorted. "This is a new one on me."

"Craig Thibodeaux, I know your kind." Madame LeBieu stuck a thick, brown finger in his face. "You be breakin' hearts all over, seein' all kinds of women, but got no love to show for it. You be showin' your loveless way for de last time." Madame LeBieu flicked her fingers, and the flames behind her leaped higher. Then, reaching inside the voluminous sleeves of the caftan, she whipped out an atomizer and sprayed a light floral scent all around him. The aroma mixed and mingled with the dark musty smells of the swamp's stagnant pools and decaying leaves.

"So you're going to douse me in perfume to unman

me?" Craig's bark of laughter clashed with the rising beat of the drums. The humor of the situation was short-lived when the mosquitoes decided they liked him even more with the added scent. Craig shook all over to discourage the beggars from landing.

"Ezili Freda Daome, Goddess of love and all dat be beautiful, listen to our prayers, accept our offerings, and enter our arms, legs, and hearts." Madame LeBieu's head dropped back, and she spread her arms wide. The drumbeat increased in intensity, reverberating off the canopy of trees shrouded in low-hanging Spanish moss.

The pounding emphasized the throbbing ache in the back of Craig's head from where Madame LeBieu's henchmen had beaned him in his room at the bait shop prior to dragging him here. The combined smells of perfume and swamp, along with the jungle beat and chanting nutcase made his stomach churn. The darkness of the night surrounded him, pushing fear into his soul.

Craig had a sudden premonition that whatever was about to happen had the potential to change his life entirely. Half of him wished they would just get on with it, whatever "it" was. The other half quaked in apprehension.

The Voodoo priestess's arms and head dropped, the drums crashing to a halt. Silence descended. Not a single cricket, frog, or bird interrupted the eerie stillness.

Craig broke the trance, fighting his growing fear with false bravado. "And I'm supposed to believe all this mumbo jumbo?" He snorted. "Give me a break. Next thing, you'll be waving a fairy wand and saying bibbity-bobbity-boo."

Madame LeBieu leveled a cold, hard stare at him.

Another shiver snaked down his spine. With the sweat dripping off his brow and chills racing down his back, he thought he might be ill. Maybe even hallucinating.

A small girl appeared at Madame LeBieu's side, handing her an ornate cup. She waited silently for the woman to drink. Craig noticed that his two former friends bowed their heads as the Voodoo lady sipped from the cup then handed it back to the girl. Clutching the cup as if it were her dearest possession, the child bowed at the waist, backing into the shadows.

With a flourishing sweep of her wrist, Madame LeBieu pulled a pastel pink, blue, and white scarf from the sleeve of her caftan, and waved it in Craig's face.

"*Mistress of Love, hear my plea.*

Help dis shameless man to see."

"You know I have family in high places, don't you?" Craig said. Not that they were there to help him now.

Madame LeBieu continued as though he hadn't spoken.

"*Though he be strong, his actions bold,*

his heart be loveless, empty, cold.

By day a frog, by night a man,

'til de next full moon, dis cunja will span."

Craig stopped shaking his head, mosquitoes be damned. What was the old lady saying? "Hey, what's this about frogs?"

"*A woman will answer Ezili's call,*

one who'll love him, warts and all."

"Who, the frog or me?" He chuckled nervously at the woman's fanatical words, downplaying his rising uneasiness. His next sarcastic statement was cut off when Mo's heavily muscled forearm crashed into his stomach. "Oomph!"

"Silence!" Mo's command warned of further retribution should Craig dare to interrupt again.

Which worked out great, since he was too busy sucking wind to restore air to his lungs. All he could do was glare at his former friend. If only looks could kill, he'd have Mo six feet under in a New Orleans minute.

Madame LeBieu went on,

"He'll watch by day and woo by night,

to gain her love, he mus fight,

to break de cunja, be whole again,

transformed into a caring man."

"You didn't have to knock the wind out of my sails." Craig wheezed, and jerked his head in Madame LeBieu's direction. "She's the one making all the noise, talking nonsense about frogs and warts."

Mo's face could have been etched in stone.

The old witch held her finger in Craig's face, forcing him to look at it. Then she drew the finger to her nose and his gaze followed until he noticed her eyes. A strange glow, having nothing to do with fire, burned in their brown-black centers. Madame LeBieu's voice dropped to a low, threatening rumble.

"Should he deny dis gift from you,

a frog he'll remain in de blackest bayou."

With a flourishing spray of perfume and one last wave of the frothy scarf, Madame LeBieu backed away from Craig, disappearing into the darkness from whence she'd come.

Craig's stomach churned and a tingling sensation spread throughout his body. He attributed his discomfort to the nauseating smells and the ropes cutting off his circulation. "Hey, you're not going to leave me here trussed up like a pig on a spit, are you?" Craig called out to the departing priestess.

A faint response carried to him from deep in the shadows. "Dôn tempt me, boy."

As soon as Madame LeBieu was gone, the men who'd stood motionless at his side throughout the Voodoo ceremony moved. They untied his bonds, grabbed him beneath the arms and hauled him back to the small canoe-like pirogue they'd brought him in.

Forced to step into the craft, Craig fell to the hard wooden seat in the middle. When the other two men climbed in, the boat rocked violently, slinging him from side to side. One man sat in front, the other at the rear. Both lifted paddles and struck out across the bayou, away from the rickety pier.

"So what's it to be now?" Craig rubbed his midsection. "Are you two going to take me out into the middle of the swamp and feed me to the alligators?" He knew these swamps as well as anyone, and the threat was real, although he didn't think Mo and Larry would do it.

Would they?

"No harm will come to you dat hasn't already been levied by Madame LeBieu," Mo said. Dropping his macho facade, he gave Craig a pitying look. "She done put de *gree gree* on you. Man, I feel sorry for you."

"Why? Because a crazy lady chanted a little mumbo jumbo and sprayed perfume in my face?" He could handle chanting crazy people. He'd represented a few of the harmless ones in the courtroom. "Don't worry about me. If I were you, I'd worry more about the monster law suit I could file against the two of you for false imprisonment."

"Going to jail would be easy compared to what you be in for." Larry's normally cheerful face wore a woeful expression.

The pale light of the half-moon shimmered between the boughs of overhanging trees. Craig could see they were headed back to his uncle's marina. Perhaps they weren't going to kill him after all. Madame LeBieu was probably just trying to scare him into leaving her granddaughter alone. No problem there. With relatives like that, he didn't need the hassle.

Besides, he'd been bored with Lisa within the first five minutes of their date. Most of the women who agreed to go out with him were only interested in what his money could buy them. Lisa had been no different.

The big Cajuns pulled up to the dock at the Thibodeaux Marina. As soon as Craig got out, they turned the boat back into the swamp, disappearing into the darkness like a fading dream.

Tired and achy, Craig trudged to his little room behind the shop, wondering if the night had been just that. A dream. He grimaced. Dream, hell. What had happened was the stuff nightmares were made of. The abrasions on his wrist confirmed it wasn't a dream, but it was over now. He would heed the warning and stay away from Madame LeBieu's granddaughter from now on.

He let himself in through the back door, flexing his sore muscles. The room was a mess from the earlier scuffle, short-lived though it was. Craig righted the night-stand and fished the alarm clock out from underneath the bed.

Without straightening the covers, he flopped onto the mattress in the tiny bedroom. It was a far cry from his suite back home, but he'd spent so many summers here as a boy, the cramped quarters didn't bother him. He was bone tired from a full day's work, a late night date gone sour, and his encounter with Madame LeBieu. What did it matter whether the sheets were of the finest linen or the cheapest cotton? A bed was a bed.

"Just another day at the office." He yawned. It would be dawn soon and his uncle expected him up bright and early to help prepare bait and fill gas tanks in the boats they rented to visiting fishermen.

Craig closed his eyes and drifted into a troubled sleep where drums beat, witches wove spells, and frogs littered the ground. A chant echoed throughout the dream, "By day a frog, by night a man, 'til the next full moon, this curse will span."

What a crock.

PROFESSOR AND RESEARCH scientist Elaine Smith moaned for the tenth time. How the staff must be laughing. Brainiac Elaine Smith, member of Mensa, valedictorian of her high school, undergraduate, *and* master's programs, with an IQ completely off the scale…and she hadn't had a clue. Until she'd opened the door to the stairwell in the science building to find her fiancé, Brian, with his hands up the shirt of a bosomy blond department secretary, while sucking out her tonsils.

The woman had seen her first, broken contact, and tapped Brian's shoulder. "Uh, this is a little awkward." She'd twittered her fingers at Elaine. "Hi, Dr. Smith."

"Elaine, I can explain," Brian had said, his hands springing free of the double-D breasts.

Without a word, Elaine had marched back to the lab. She'd only been away for a moment. If the drink machine on the second floor had worked, she wouldn't have opened that door. Thank God she'd made this discovery before she'd been even more idiotic and married the creep.

She crossed the shiny white floor to her desk and ran her hand over her favorite microscope, letting the coolness of the metal seep into her flushed skin. With careful precision, she poured a drop from the glass jar marked Bayou Miste onto a slide. With another clean slide, she smeared the sample across the glass, and slid it beneath the scope.

The routine process of studying microorganisms calmed her like no other tonic. Her heartbeat slowed and she lost herself in the beauty of microbiology. She didn't have to think about the world outside the science department. Many times in her life, she'd escaped behind lab doors to avoid the ugly side of society.

"Elaine the brain. Elaine the brain." Echoes of children's' taunts from long ago plagued her attempts at serenity.

Elaine snorted. *Wouldn't they laugh, now? Elaine-the-brain, too stupid to live.*

A tear dropped onto the lens of the microscope, blurring her view, and the lab door burst open. She scrubbed her hand across her eyes before she looked up. She'd be damned if she'd let the jerk see her cry.

"Elaine, let me explain." Brian strode in, a sufficiently contrite expression on his face.

He'd probably practiced the expression in the mirror to make it look so real. Elaine wasn't buying it. She forced her voice to be flat and disinterested. "Brian, I'm busy."

"We have to talk."

"No...we don't." She turned her back to him, her chest tight and her stomach clenching.

"Look, I'm sorry." Brian's voice didn't sound convincing. "It's just...well...ah, hell. I needed more."

Her mouth dropped open and she spun to face him. "More what? More women? More conquests? More sex in the hallways?"

He dug his hands in his pocket and scuffed his black leather shoe on the white tile. When he looked up, a corner of his mouth lifted and his gray eyes appeared sad. "I needed to know I was more important than a specimen, that I was wanted for more than just a convenient companion."

"So you made out with a secretary in the stairwell?"

"She at least pays attention to me." When she spun away, he grabbed her arm. "I should have broken our engagement first, but every time I tried, you'd bury yourself in this lab." He ran a hand through his hair and stepped closer. "It would never have worked between us. I couldn't compete with your first love."

"What are you talking about?"

218

"Your obsession with science." He inhaled deeply and looked at the corner ceiling, before his gaze came back to her. "Face it, Elaine, you love science more than you ever loved me."

"No, I don't." Her denial was swift, followed closely by the thought *'Do I?'*

He crossed his arms over his chest and stood with his feet spread slightly. "Then say it."

"Say what?"

"Say, I love you." He stood still waiting for her response.

She summoned righteous indignation, puffed out her chest and prepared to say the words he'd asked for. She opened her mouth, but the words stuck in her throat like a nasty-tasting wad of guilt. Instead of saying anything, she exhaled.

Had she ever really loved Brian? She studied his rounded face and curly blond hair. He had the geek-boy-next-door look, and he'd made her smile on occasion. She'd enjoyed the feeling of having someone to call her own, and to fill the lonely gap in her everyday existence. She hadn't had anyone in her life, no one to turn to since her parents had died four years ago. Having grown up too smart to fit in with kids her own age, she'd missed the much needed education only peers could provide and she didn't have any close friends. Had she wanted too much from Brian?

Had she really loved him? After all the years of living in relative isolation from any meaningful relationships, was she even capable of feeling love?

Her chest felt as empty as her roiling stomach. He was

right. She couldn't say she loved him when she knew those words were a lie. And as much as she didn't like conflict, she disliked lying more.

How long had she been deluding herself into thinking they were the perfect couple?

"It's no use, Elaine. Our marriage would be a huge mistake. The only way you'd notice me is if I were a specimen under your microscope. It's not enough. I need more. I need someone who isn't afraid to get out and experience the world beyond this lab."

He turned and walked out, leaving a quiet room full of scientific equipment—and one very confused woman.

Afraid to get out? She glanced around the stark clean walls of the laboratory, the one place she could escape to when she wanted to feel safe.

Dear God, why can't I be like normal people? Brian was right. She felt more comfortable behind the lab door than in the world outside.

When she stared down at the litter of items on the table, blinking to clear the tears from her eyes, she spied the jar labeled Bayou Miste. The container had come to her in the mail, an anonymous sample of Louisiana swamp water. She stood, momentarily transfixed by the sight of the plain mason jar, a strange thrumming sound echoing in her subconscious, almost like drums beating. Probably some punk in the parking lot with his woofers too loud.

With an odd sense of fate, she leaned over the microscope, dried her tear from the lens with a tissue, and studied the slide. Her skin tingled and her heartbeat amplified. Here was her opportunity to get away from the lab.

She could help solve the pollution problems of an ecosystem, even if she couldn't solve the microcosm of her love life.

ABOUT THE AUTHOR

ELLE JAMES also writing as MYLA JACKSON is a *New York Times* and *USA Today* Bestselling author of books including cowboys, intrigues and paranormal adventures that keep her readers on the edges of their seats. When she's not at her computer, she's traveling, snow skiing, boating, or riding her ATV, dreaming up new stories. Learn more about Elle James at www.ellejames.com

Website | Facebook | Twitter | GoodReads | Newsletter | BookBub | Amazon

Or visit her alter ego Myla Jackson at mylajackson.com
Website | Facebook | Twitter | Newsletter

Follow Me!
www.ellejames.com
ellejames@ellejames.com

ALSO BY ELLE JAMES

Up in Flames (#6)

Total Meltdown (#7) TBD

Declan's Defenders

Marine Force Recon (#1)

Show of Force (#2)

Full Force (#3)

Driving Force (#4)

Mission: Six

One Intrepid SEAL

Two Dauntless Hearts

Three Courageous Words

Four Relentless Days

Five Ways to Surrender

Six Minutes to Midnight

Hearts & Heroes Series

Wyatt's War (#1)

Mack's Witness (#2)

Ronin's Return (#3)

Sam's Surrender (#4)

Take No Prisoners Series

SEAL's Honor (#1)

SEAL'S Desire (#2)

SEAL's Embrace (#3)

SEAL's Obsession (#4)

SEAL's Proposal (#5)

SEAL's Seduction (#6)

SEAL'S Defiance (#7)

SEAL's Deception (#8)

SEAL's Deliverance (#9)

SEAL's Ultimate Challenge (#10)

Texas Billionaire Club

Tarzan & Janine (#1)

Something To Talk About (#2)

Who's Your Daddy (#3)

Love & War (#4)

Ballistic Cowboy

Hot Combat (#1)

Hot Target (#2)

Hot Zone (#3)

Hot Velocity (#4)

Cajun Magic Mystery Series

Voodoo on the Bayou (#1)

Voodoo for Two (#2)

Deja Voodoo (#3)

Cajun Magic Mysteries Books 1-3

Billionaire Online Dating Service

The Billionaire Husband Test (#1)

The Billionaire Cinderella Test (#2)

The Billionaire Bride Test (#3)

The Billionaire Matchmaker Test (#4)

SEAL Of My Own

Navy SEAL Survival

Navy SEAL Captive

Navy SEAL To Die For

Navy SEAL Six Pack

Devil's Shroud Series

Deadly Reckoning (#1)

Deadly Engagement (#2)

Deadly Liaisons (#3)

Deadly Allure (#4)

Deadly Obsession (#5)

Deadly Fall (#6)

Covert Cowboys Inc Series

Triggered (#1)

Taking Aim (#2)

Bodyguard Under Fire (#3)

Cowboy Resurrected (#4)

Navy SEAL Justice (#5)

Navy SEAL Newlywed (#6)

High Country Hideout (#7)

Clandestine Christmas (#8)

Thunder Horse Series

Hostage to Thunder Horse (#1)

Thunder Horse Heritage (#2)

Thunder Horse Redemption (#3)

Christmas at Thunder Horse Ranch (#4)

Demon Series

Hot Demon Nights (#1)

Demon's Embrace (#2)

Tempting the Demon (#3)

Lords of the Underworld

Witch's Initiation (#1)

Witch's Seduction (#2)

The Witch's Desire (#3)

Possessing the Witch (#4)

Stealth Operations Specialists (SOS)

Nick of Time

Alaskan Fantasy

Blown Away

Feel the Heat

The Heart of a Cowboy

Protecting His Heroine

Warrior's Conquest

Rogues

Enslaved by the Viking Short Story

Conquests

Smokin' Hot Firemen

Love on the Rocks

Protecting the Colton Bride

Heir to Murder

Secret Service Rescue

High Octane Heroes

Haunted

Engaged with the Boss

Cowboy Brigade

Time Raiders: The Whisper

Bundle of Trouble

Killer Body

Operation XOXO

An Unexpected Clue

Baby Bling

Under Suspicion, With Child

Texas-Size Secrets

Cowboy Sanctuary

Lakota Baby

Dakota Meltdown

Beneath the Texas Moon

Made in the USA
Monee, IL
07 March 2024

54621559R10134